STONE ARCH BOOKS
a capstone imprint

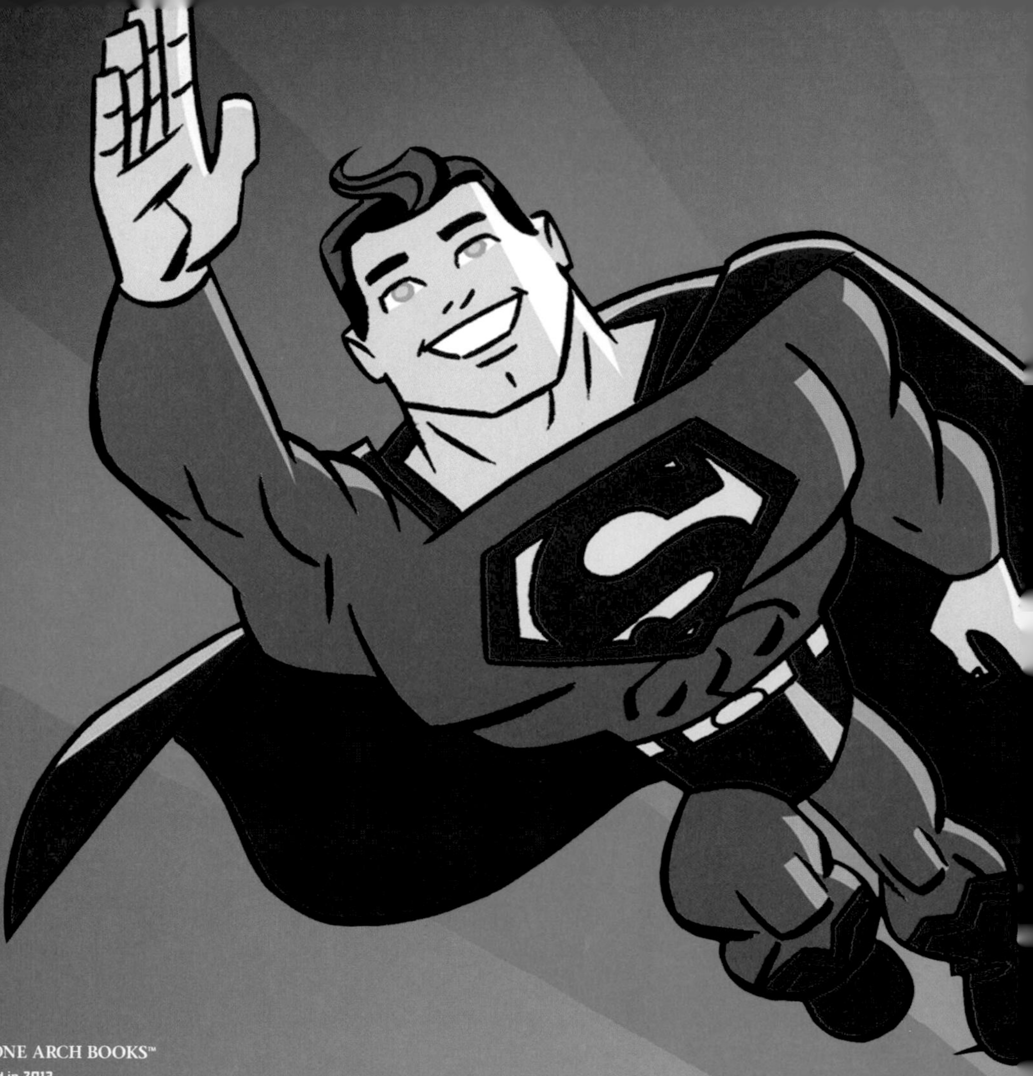

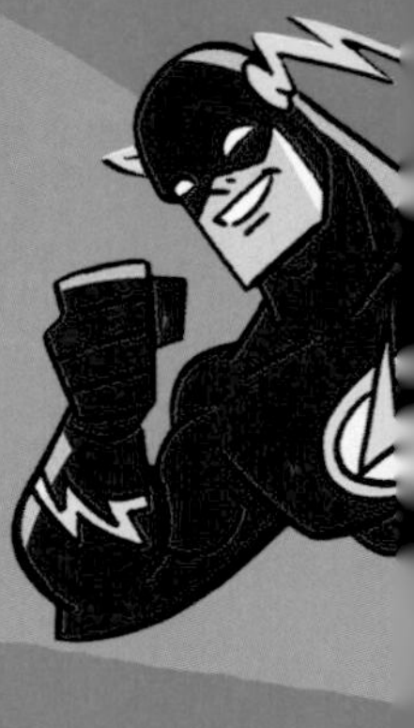

STONE ARCH BOOKS™
Published in 2013
A Capstone Imprint
1710 Roe Crest Drive
North Mankato, MN 56003
www.capstonepub.com

Originally published by DC Comics in
the U.S. in single magazine form as
DC Super Friends #6.

Cataloging-in-Publication Data is available at the
Library of Congress website:
ISBN: 978-1-4342-4701-8 (library binding)

Summary: You're invited to a special day: The
Challenge of The Super Friends! Thrill as our heroes
design special traps for each other at a charity event.
Chill as those traps are sabotaged by the Key! How
will they escape?

STONE ARCH BOOKS
Ashley C. Andersen Zantop *Publisher*
Michael Dahl *Editorial Director*
Donald Lemke & Julie Gassman *Editors*
Heather Kindseth *Creative Director*
Brann Garvey *Designer*
Kathy McColley *Production Specialist*

DC COMICS
Rachel Gluckstern *Original U.S. Editor*

Printed in China by Nordica.
1012/CA21201277
092012 006935NORDS13

DC Comics
1700 Broadway, New York, NY 10019
A Warner Bros. Entertainment Company

DC Super Friends

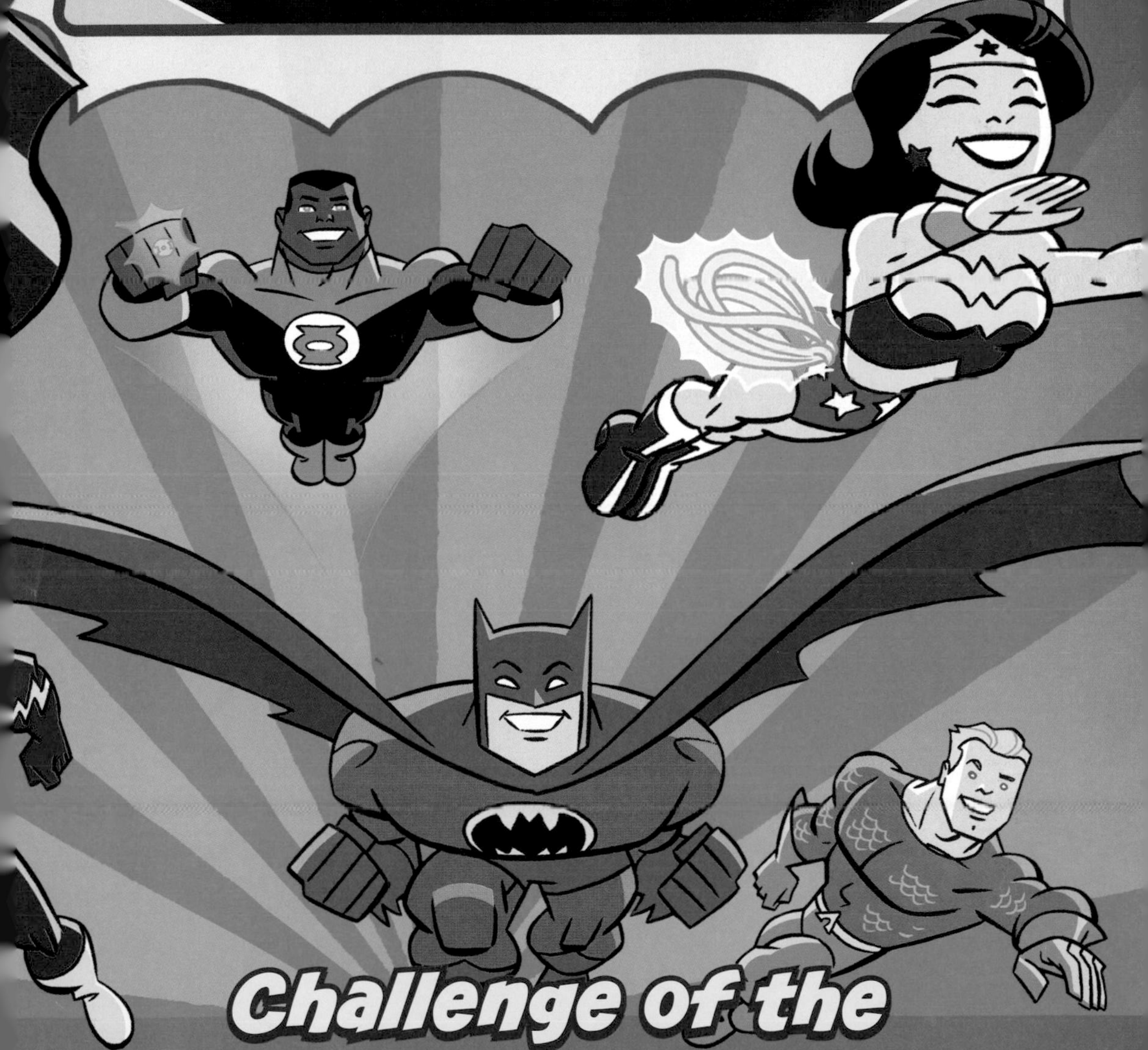

Challenge of the Super friends

Sholly Fisch ....writer
Dario Brizuela.........................artist
Heroic Age .... colorist
Randy Gentile ....letterer
J. Bone ....cover artist

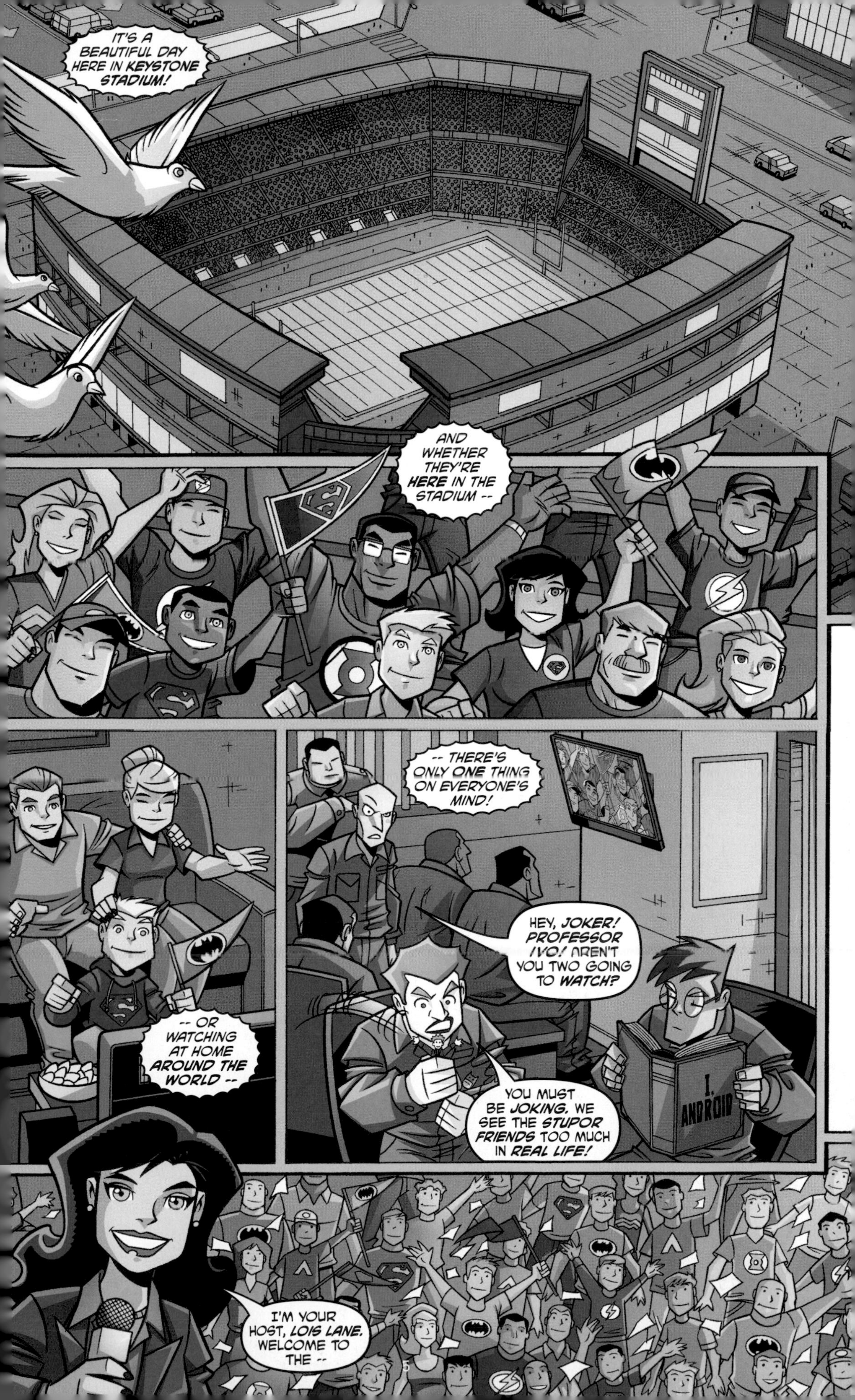
IT'S A BEAUTIFUL DAY HERE IN KEYSTONE STADIUM!
AND WHETHER THEY'RE HERE IN THE STADIUM --
-- OR WATCHING AT HOME AROUND THE WORLD --
-- THERE'S ONLY ONE THING ON EVERYONE'S MIND!
HEY, JOKER! PROFESSOR IVO! AREN'T YOU TWO GOING TO WATCH?
I, ANDROID
YOU MUST BE JOKING. WE SEE THE STUPOR FRIENDS TOO MUCH IN REAL LIFE!
I'M YOUR HOST, LOIS LANE. WELCOME TO THE --

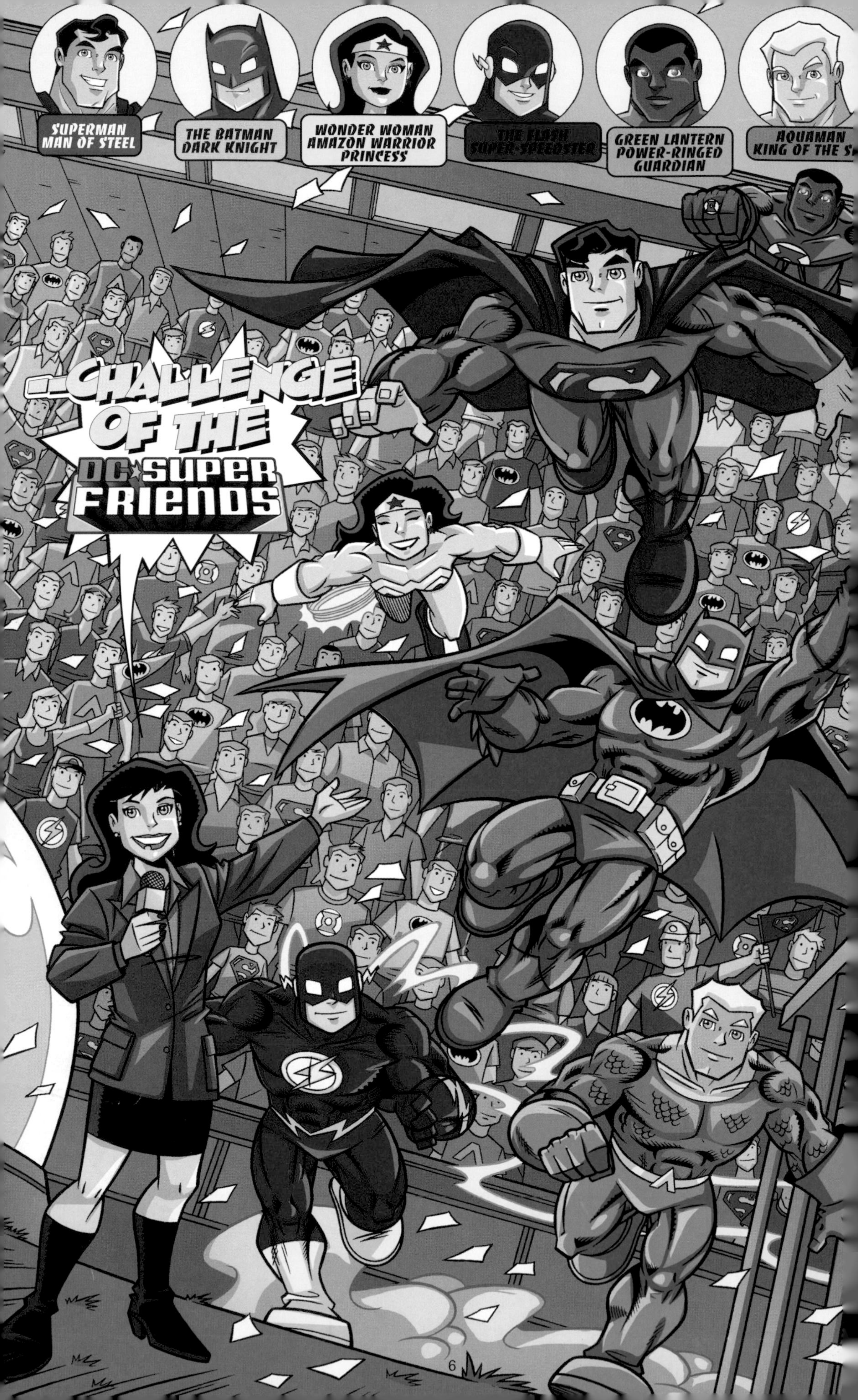
SUPERMAN
MAN OF STEEL
THE BATMAN
DARK KNIGHT
WONDER WOMAN
AMAZON WARRIOR
PRINCESS
THE FLASH
SUPER-SPEEDSTER
GREEN LANTERN
POWER-RINGED
GUARDIAN
AQUAMAN
KING OF THE
CHALLENGE OF THE
DC SUPER FRIENDS

SUPERMAN, CAN YOU *EXPLAIN* THE CHALLENGE TO OUR AUDIENCE?

I'LL BE HAPPY TO.

VILLAINS ARE *ALWAYS* SETTING TRAPS FOR THE SUPER FRIENDS. BUT WE ALWAYS FIND A WAY TO *ESCAPE* AND CATCH THEM.

THAT GAVE US AN *IDEA.*

WHY NOT TURN IT INTO A *CONTEST* AND RAISE MONEY FOR *CHARITY?* SO WE BUILT THESE TRAPS FOR *EACH OTHER.*

EACH TRAP HAS *ONE* BUILT-IN WAY TO ESCAPE. OUR CHALLENGE IS TO *FIND* IT AND BE THE *FIRST* TO GET OUT!

ONLY *ONE* WAY OUT? THAT DOESN'T SOUND *EASY.*

IT *WON'T* BE! AND TO MAKE IT HARDER, WE'RE NOT ALLOWED TO USE ANY *GADGETS* OR *TOOLS.* ALL WE CAN USE IS OUR *ABILITIES* AND OUR *BRAINS!*

THANK YOU, *SUPERMAN!*

WELL, I CAN SEE THE SUPER FRIENDS ARE READY TO *BEGIN.* SO LET'S TAKE A LOOK AT THE TRAPS THEY'LL FACE.

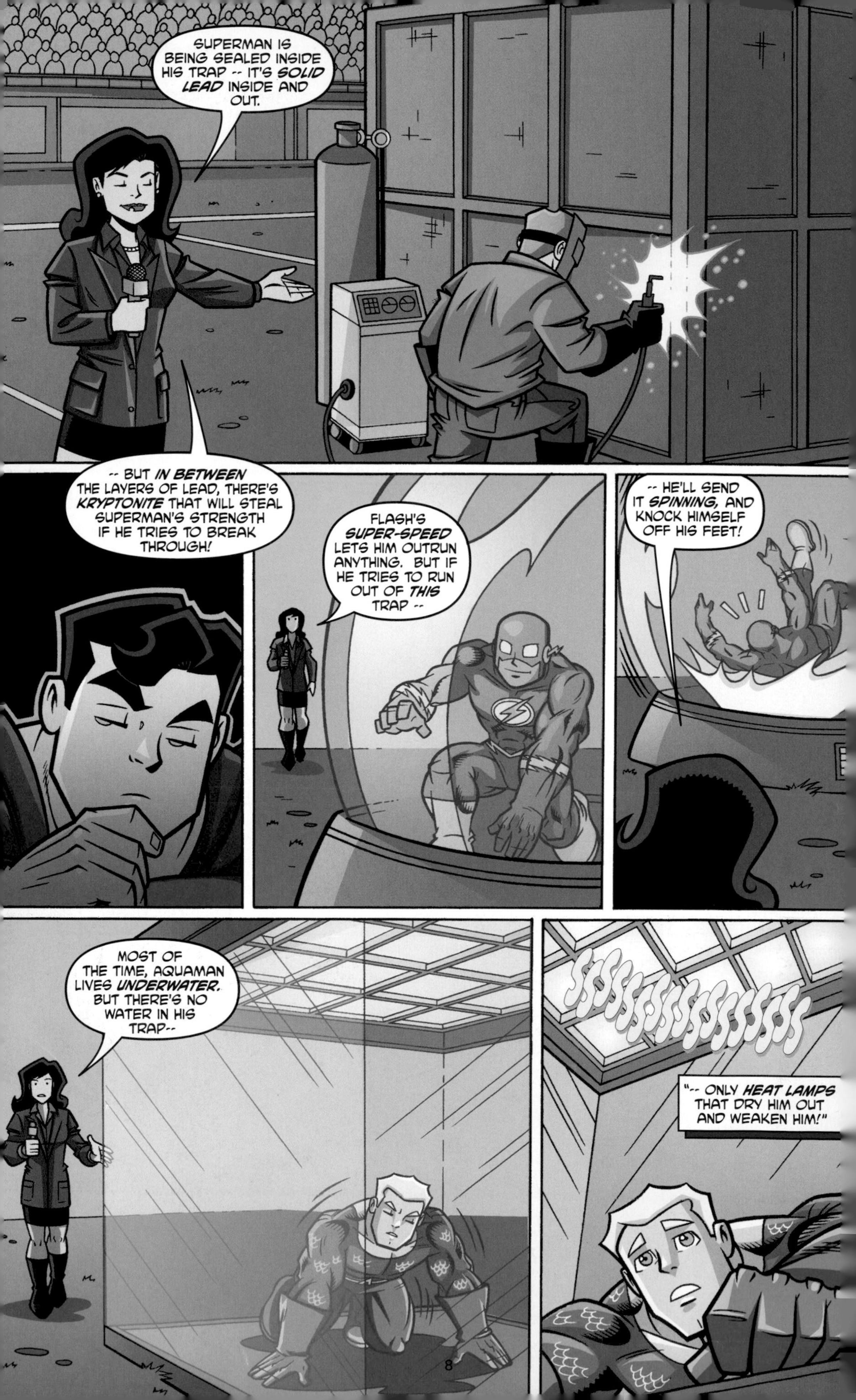

SUPERMAN IS BEING SEALED INSIDE HIS TRAP -- IT'S SOLID LEAD INSIDE AND OUT.
-- BUT IN BETWEEN THE LAYERS OF LEAD, THERE'S KRYPTONITE THAT WILL STEAL SUPERMAN'S STRENGTH IF HE TRIES TO BREAK THROUGH!
FLASH'S SUPER-SPEED LETS HIM OUTRUN ANYTHING. BUT IF HE TRIES TO RUN OUT OF THIS TRAP --
-- HE'LL SEND IT SPINNING, AND KNOCK HIMSELF OFF HIS FEET!
MOST OF THE TIME, AQUAMAN LIVES UNDERWATER. BUT THERE'S NO WATER IN HIS TRAP--
SSSSSSSSSSSSSSSSSSSS
"-- ONLY HEAT LAMPS THAT DRY HIM OUT AND WEAKEN HIM!"

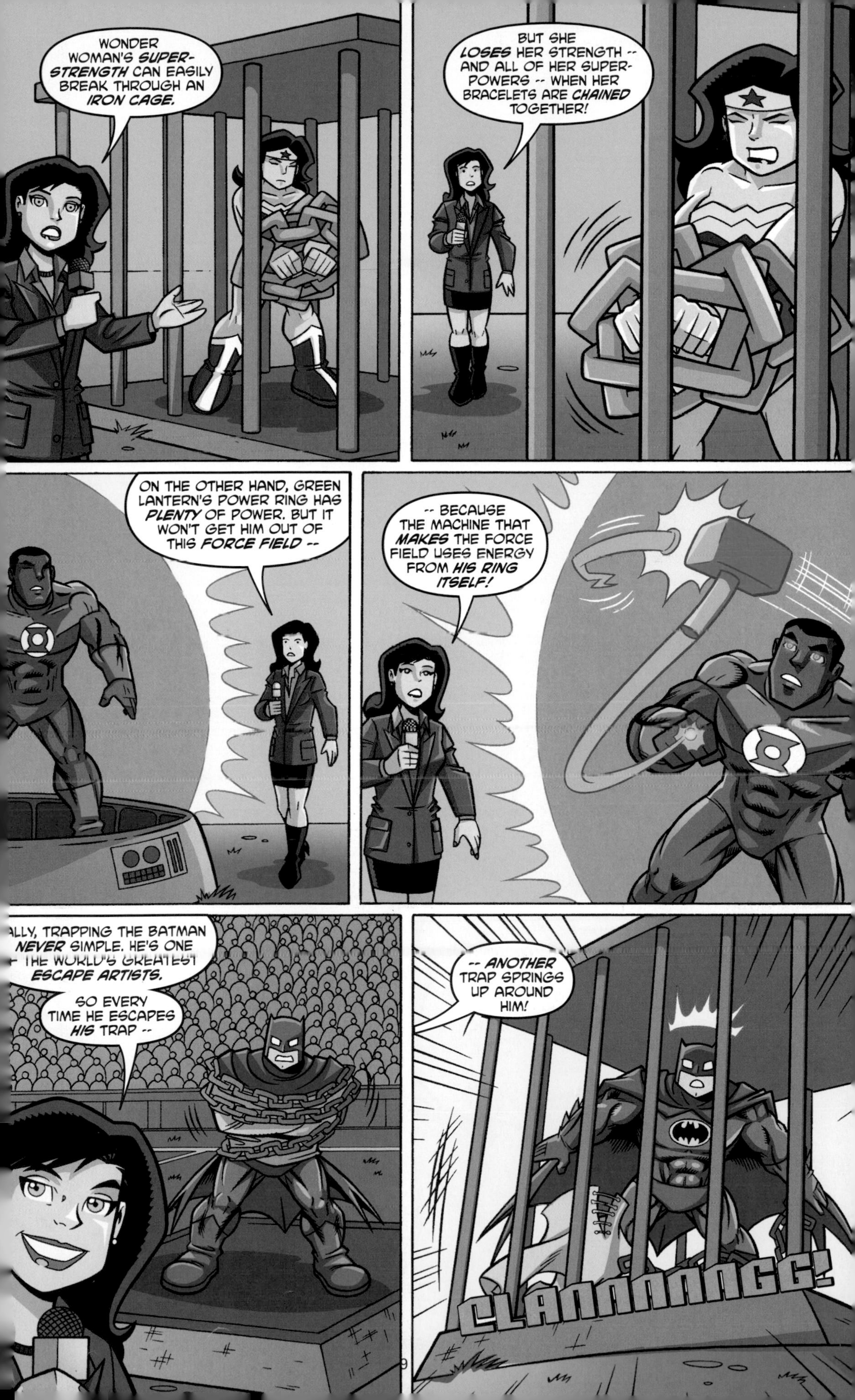
WONDER WOMAN'S SUPER-STRENGTH CAN EASILY BREAK THROUGH AN IRON CAGE.
BUT SHE LOSES HER STRENGTH -- AND ALL OF HER SUPER-POWERS -- WHEN HER BRACELETS ARE CHAINED TOGETHER!
ON THE OTHER HAND, GREEN LANTERN'S POWER RING HAS PLENTY OF POWER. BUT IT WON'T GET HIM OUT OF THIS FORCE FIELD --
-- BECAUSE THE MACHINE THAT MAKES THE FORCE FIELD USES ENERGY FROM HIS RING ITSELF!
ALLY, TRAPPING THE BATMAN NEVER SIMPLE. HE'S ONE THE WORLD'S GREATEST ESCAPE ARTISTS.
SO EVERY TIME HE ESCAPES HIS TRAP --
-- ANOTHER TRAP SPRINGS UP AROUND HIM!
CLANNNNNNGG!

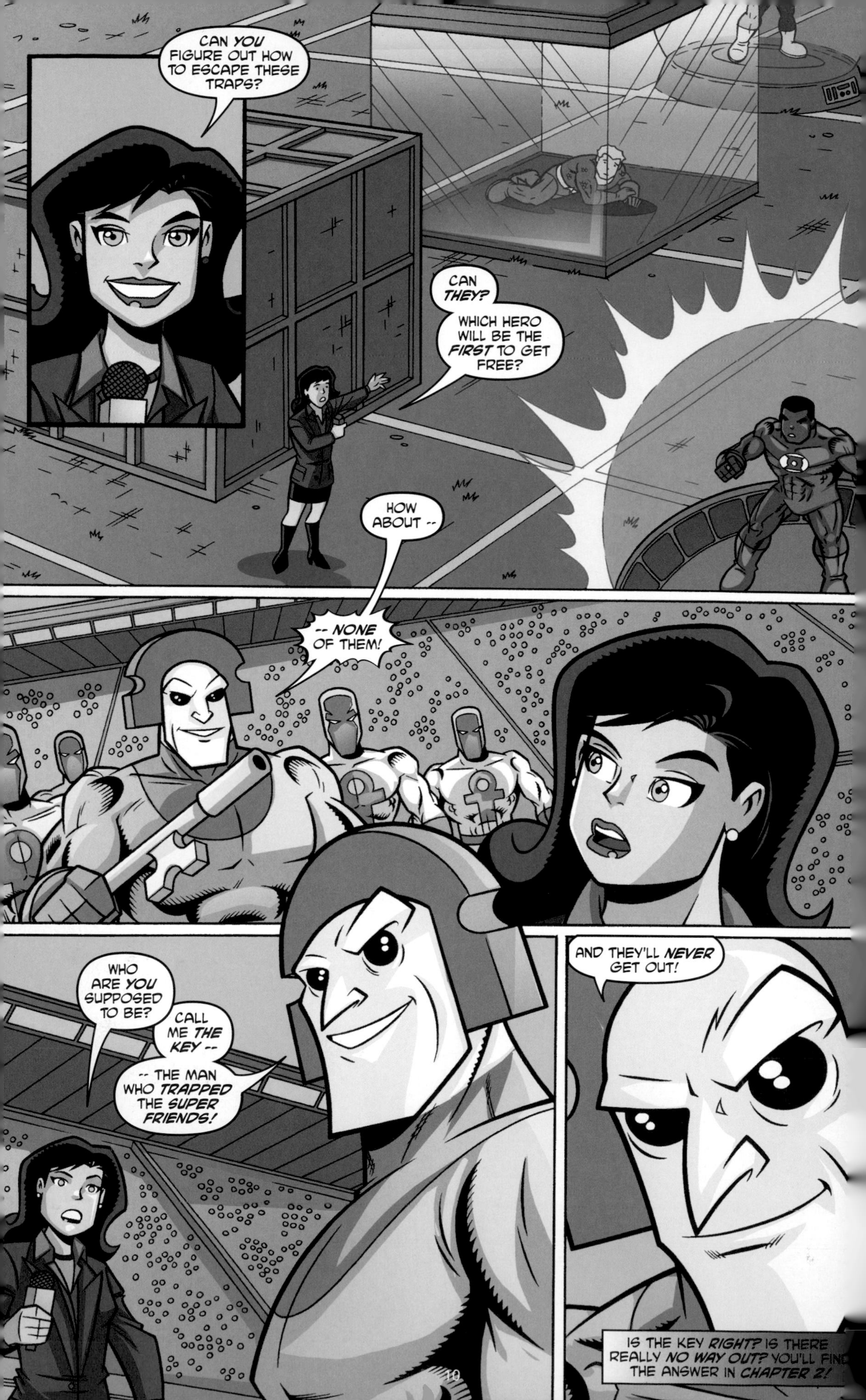
CAN YOU FIGURE OUT HOW TO ESCAPE THESE TRAPS?
CAN THEY?
WHICH HERO WILL BE THE FIRST TO GET FREE?
HOW ABOUT --
-- NONE OF THEM!
WHO ARE YOU SUPPOSED TO BE?
CALL ME THE KEY --
-- THE MAN WHO TRAPPED THE SUPER FRIENDS!
AND THEY'LL NEVER GET OUT!
IS THE KEY RIGHT? IS THERE REALLY NO WAY OUT? YOU'LL FIND THE ANSWER IN CHAPTER 2!

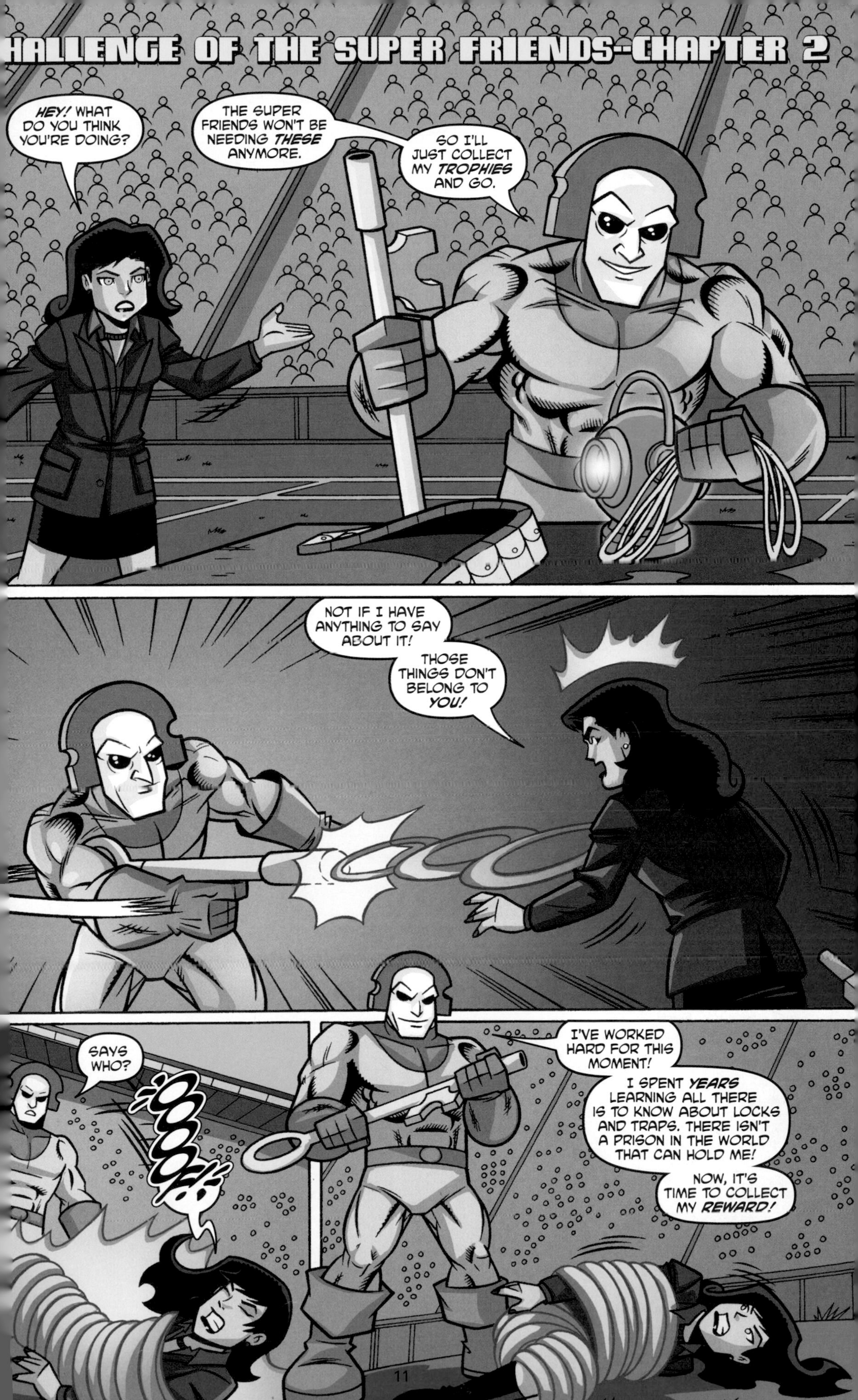
CHALLENGE OF THE SUPER FRIENDS--CHAPTER 2
HEY! WHAT DO YOU THINK YOU'RE DOING?
THE SUPER FRIENDS WON'T BE NEEDING THESE ANYMORE.
SO I'LL JUST COLLECT MY TROPHIES AND GO.
NOT IF I HAVE ANYTHING TO SAY ABOUT IT!
THOSE THINGS DON'T BELONG TO YOU!
SAYS WHO?
OOOF!
I'VE WORKED HARD FOR THIS MOMENT!
I SPENT YEARS LEARNING ALL THERE IS TO KNOW ABOUT LOCKS AND TRAPS. THERE ISN'T A PRISON IN THE WORLD THAT CAN HOLD ME!
NOW, IT'S TIME TO COLLECT MY REWARD!

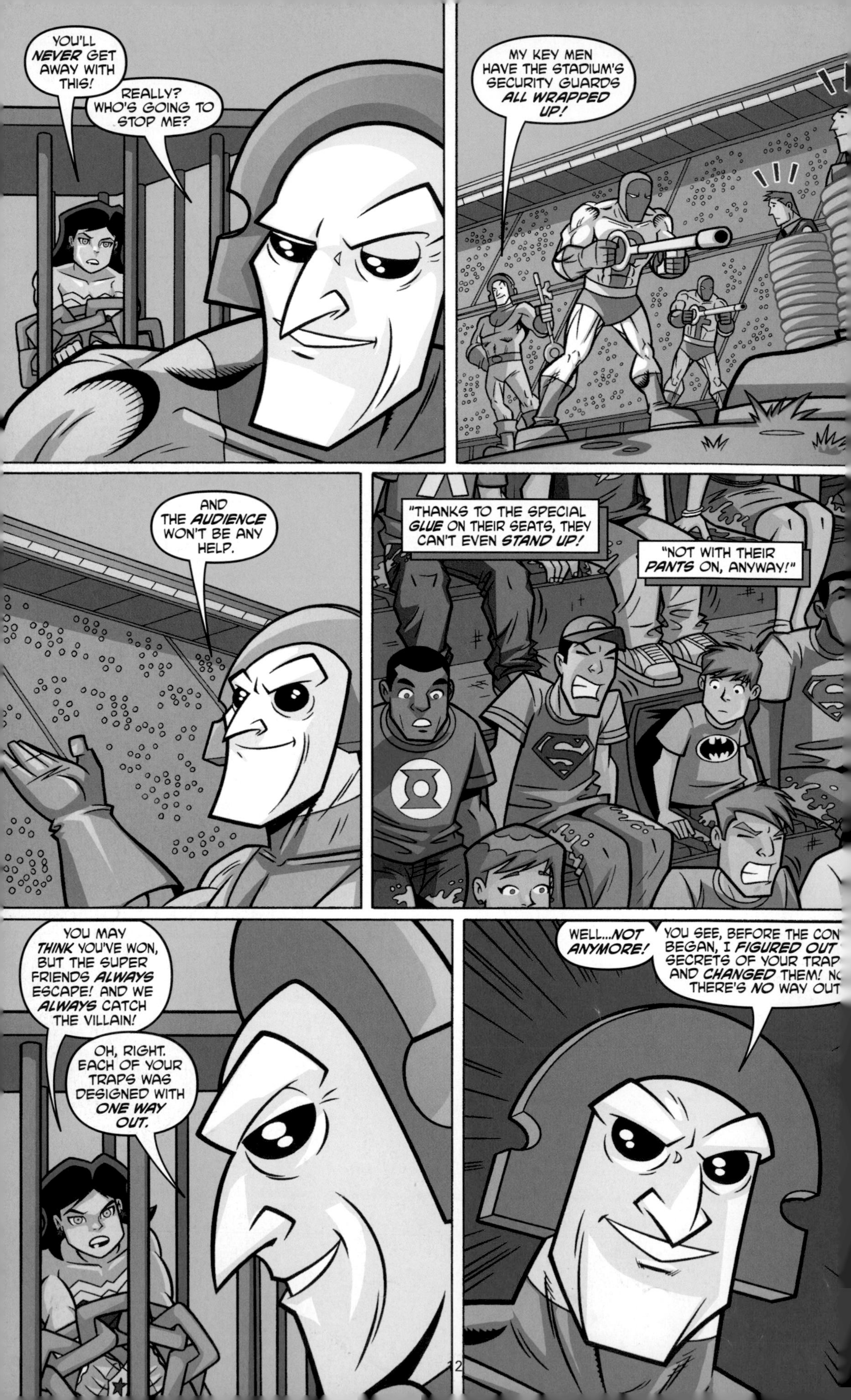
YOU'LL NEVER GET AWAY WITH THIS!
REALLY? WHO'S GOING TO STOP ME?
MY KEY MEN HAVE THE STADIUM'S SECURITY GUARDS ALL WRAPPED UP!
AND THE AUDIENCE WON'T BE ANY HELP.
"THANKS TO THE SPECIAL GLUE ON THEIR SEATS, THEY CAN'T EVEN STAND UP!
"NOT WITH THEIR PANTS ON, ANYWAY!"
YOU MAY THINK YOU'VE WON, BUT THE SUPER FRIENDS ALWAYS ESCAPE! AND WE ALWAYS CATCH THE VILLAIN!
OH, RIGHT. EACH OF YOUR TRAPS WAS DESIGNED WITH ONE WAY OUT.
WELL...NOT ANYMORE!
YOU SEE, BEFORE THE CON BEGAN, I FIGURED OUT SECRETS OF YOUR TRAP AND CHANGED THEM! N THERE'S NO WAY OUT

WITH YOUR SUPER-STRENGTH *GONE*, YOUR ONLY WAY OUT WOULD BE TO USE YOUR AMAZON TIARA TO *SAW* THROUGH THE CHAIN.

TOO BAD I REPLACED YOUR CHAIN WITH A MUCH *THICKER* ONE -- THICK ENOUGH TO HOLD A *BATTLESHIP!*

IT WOULD TAKE YOU *WEEKS* TO SAW THROUGH IT!

THE ENERGY FOR *GREEN LANTERN'S* TRAP COMES FROM HIS *RING*. SO, IF HE LETS HIS RING *RUN OUT* OF POWER, THE FORCE FIELD SHOULD *DISAPPEAR*.

POWER LEVEL ZERO.

BUT I ADDED A *BACK-UP* POWER SOURCE. NOW, EVEN *AFTER* HIS RING IS EMPTY, THE TRAP STAYS AS STRONG AS EVER!

SUPERMAN'S FRIENDS MIGHT *SAY* THEY LINED HIS TRAP WITH KRYPTONITE, BUT THEY WOULDN'T *REALLY* DO IT.

I WOULD, THOUGH.

THE FLASH CAN'T RUN INSIDE HIS SPHERE, BUT HE COULD SIT DOWN AND VIBRATE HIS BODY RIGHT THROUGH THE FLOOR.

EXCEPT THAT I RIGGED THE SPHERE TO VIBRATE WHENEVER *HE* DOES. SO NOW, HE JUST GETS *ALL SHAKEN UP!*

AQUAMAN COULD HAVE *BROKEN* THE HEAT *LAMPS* BY PULLING OUT THEIR WIRES --

-- SO I ADDED *MORE* LAMPS, TO MAKE HIM TOO WEAK TO DO IT!

AND *THE BATMAN* MIGHT BE GREAT AT ESCAPING FROM *ROPES* OR PICKING *LOCKS* --

-- BUT HOW ABOUT WHEN HE'S BURIED UP TO HIS *NECK* IN *QUICK-DRYING CEMENT?*

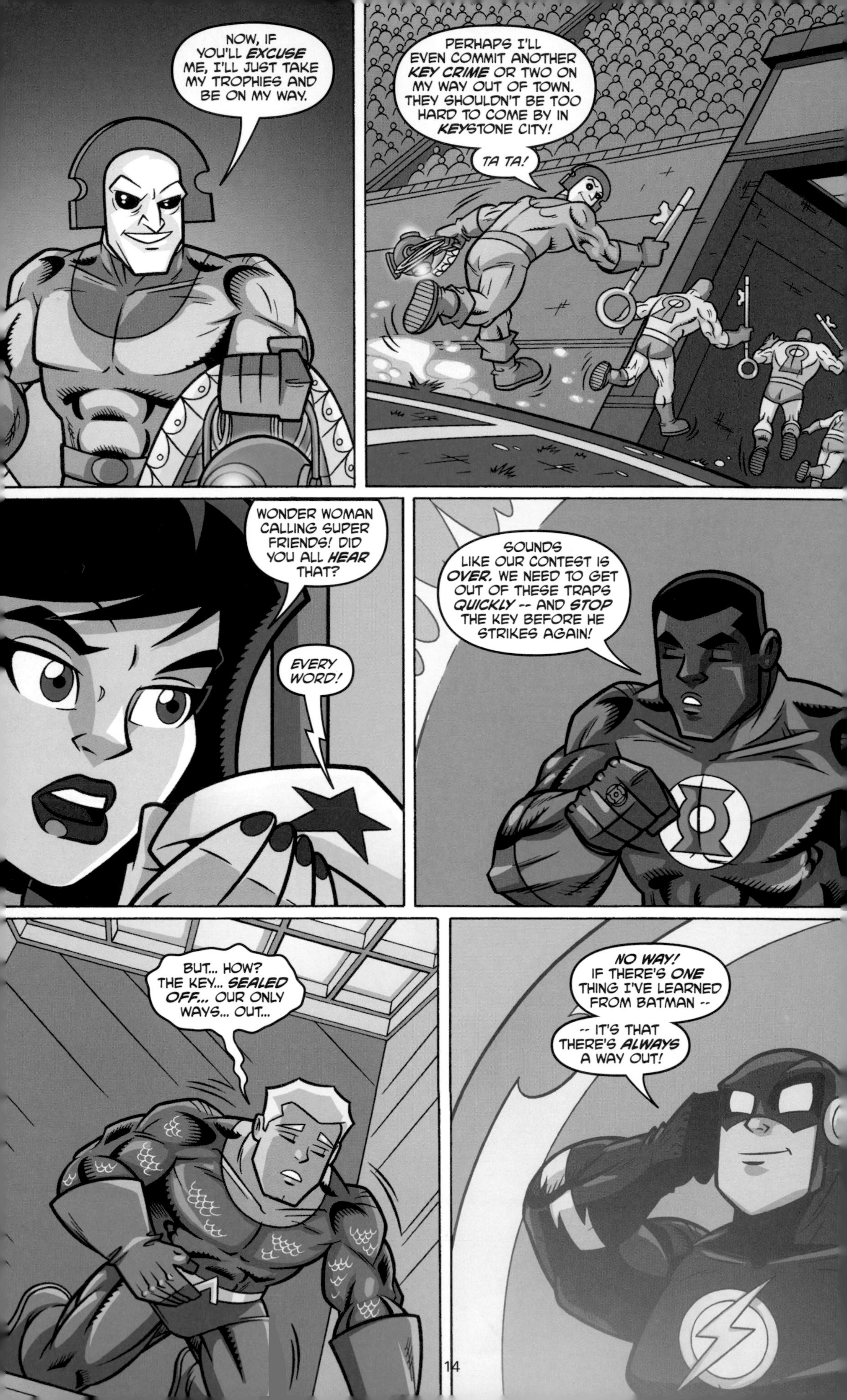
NOW, IF YOU'LL EXCUSE ME, I'LL JUST TAKE MY TROPHIES AND BE ON MY WAY.
PERHAPS I'LL EVEN COMMIT ANOTHER KEY CRIME OR TWO ON MY WAY OUT OF TOWN. THEY SHOULDN'T BE TOO HARD TO COME BY IN KEYSTONE CITY!
TA TA!
WONDER WOMAN CALLING SUPER FRIENDS! DID YOU ALL HEAR THAT?
EVERY WORD!
SOUNDS LIKE OUR CONTEST IS OVER. WE NEED TO GET OUT OF THESE TRAPS QUICKLY -- AND STOP THE KEY BEFORE HE STRIKES AGAIN!
BUT... HOW? THE KEY... SEALED OFF... OUR ONLY WAYS... OUT...
NO WAY! IF THERE'S ONE THING I'VE LEARNED FROM BATMAN --
-- IT'S THAT THERE'S ALWAYS A WAY OUT!

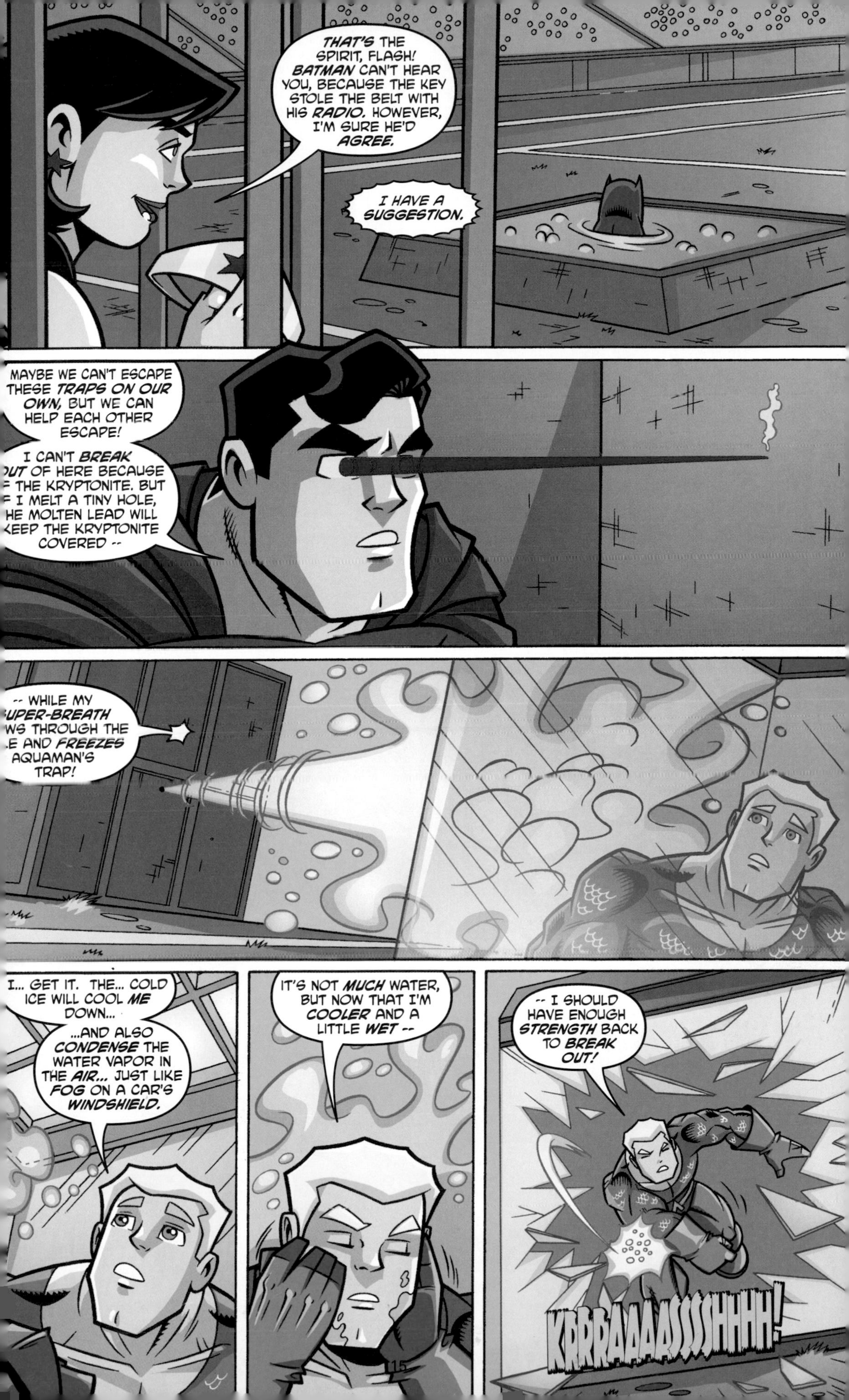
THAT'S THE SPIRIT, FLASH! BATMAN CAN'T HEAR YOU, BECAUSE THE KEY STOLE THE BELT WITH HIS RADIO. HOWEVER, I'M SURE HE'D AGREE.
I HAVE A SUGGESTION.
MAYBE WE CAN'T ESCAPE THESE TRAPS ON OUR OWN, BUT WE CAN HELP EACH OTHER ESCAPE!
I CAN'T BREAK UT OF HERE BECAUSE F THE KRYPTONITE. BUT F I MELT A TINY HOLE, HE MOLTEN LEAD WILL EEP THE KRYPTONITE COVERED --
-- WHILE MY UPER-BREATH WS THROUGH THE E AND FREEZES AQUAMAN'S TRAP!
I... GET IT. THE... COLD ICE WILL COOL ME DOWN...
...AND ALSO CONDENSE THE WATER VAPOR IN THE AIR... JUST LIKE FOG ON A CAR'S WINDSHIELD.
IT'S NOT MUCH WATER, BUT NOW THAT I'M COOLER AND A LITTLE WET --
-- I SHOULD HAVE ENOUGH STRENGTH BACK TO BREAK OUT!
KRRRAAAASSSSHHHH!

NOW, TO RETURN THE FAVOR --

-- BY *JAMMING* THE FLASH'S TRAP SO THAT IT CAN'T *TURN!*

COOL! THAT'S ALL I NEED TO WHIP UP A *SUPER-SPEED TORNADO* AND BUST OUT!

WHOOOOSSSSSHHHH!

SPEAKING OF WHICH...

DID YOU KNOW THAT A *HURRICANE* CAN BLOW FAST ENOUGH TO DRIVE A *STRAW* STRAIGHT THROUGH AN *OAK TREE?*

WITH ENOUGH *SPEED,* I BET IT WORKS FOR *AMAZON TIARAS* AND *CHAINS,* TOO!

GREAT HERA! I FEEL MY POWERS RETURNING!

WITH MY STRENGTH *RESTORED* --

KRANNGG!

-- I WILL BE *FREE!*

SKREEELLNNNNCHHH!

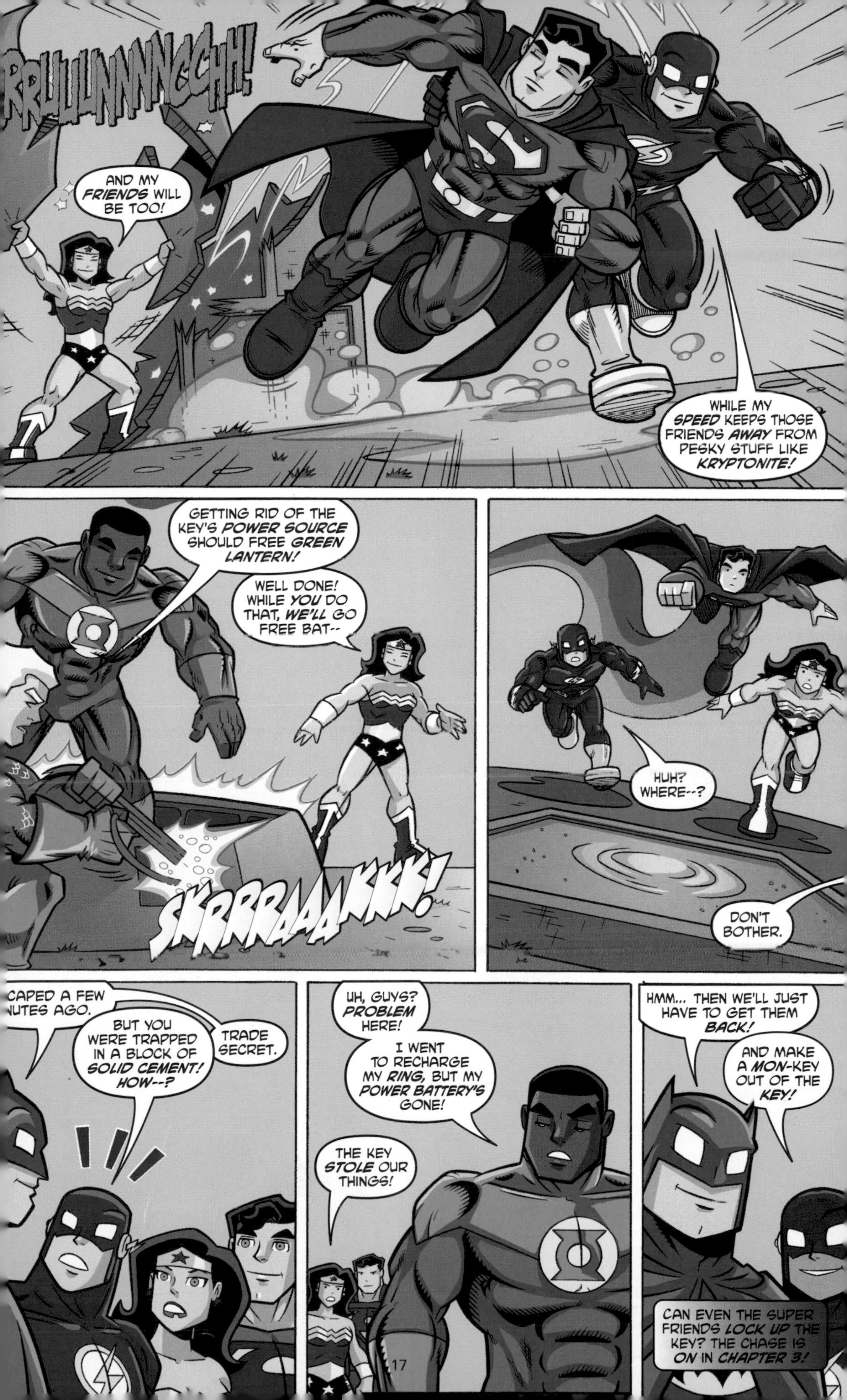
RRUUUNNNNGCHH!
AND MY FRIENDS WILL BE TOO!
WHILE MY SPEED KEEPS THOSE FRIENDS AWAY FROM PESKY STUFF LIKE KRYPTONITE!
GETTING RID OF THE KEY'S POWER SOURCE SHOULD FREE GREEN LANTERN!
WELL DONE! WHILE YOU DO THAT, WE'LL GO FREE BAT--
SKRRRAAAKKK!
HUH? WHERE--?
DON'T BOTHER.
CAPED A FEW NUTES AGO.
BUT YOU WERE TRAPPED IN A BLOCK OF SOLID CEMENT! HOW--?
TRADE SECRET.
!!!
UH, GUYS? PROBLEM HERE!
I WENT TO RECHARGE MY RING, BUT MY POWER BATTERY'S GONE!
THE KEY STOLE OUR THINGS!
HMM... THEN WE'LL JUST HAVE TO GET THEM BACK!
AND MAKE A MON-KEY OUT OF THE KEY!
CAN EVEN THE SUPER FRIENDS LOCK UP THE KEY? THE CHASE IS ON IN CHAPTER 3!

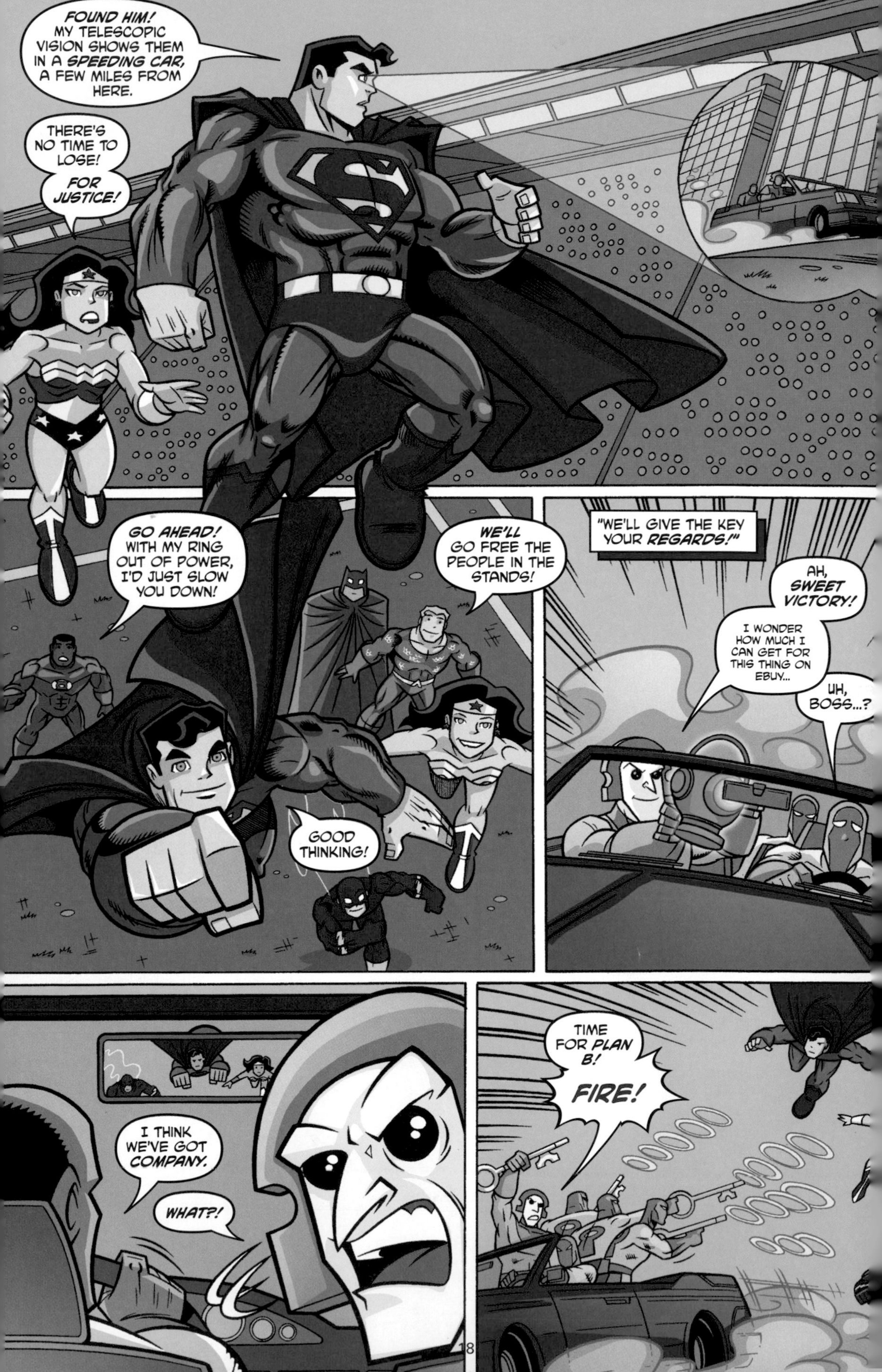
FOUND HIM! MY TELESCOPIC VISION SHOWS THEM IN A SPEEDING CAR, A FEW MILES FROM HERE.
THERE'S NO TIME TO LOSE!
FOR JUSTICE!
GO AHEAD! WITH MY RING OUT OF POWER, I'D JUST SLOW YOU DOWN!
WE'LL GO FREE THE PEOPLE IN THE STANDS!
GOOD THINKING!
"WE'LL GIVE THE KEY YOUR REGARDS!"
AH, SWEET VICTORY!
I WONDER HOW MUCH I CAN GET FOR THIS THING ON EBUY...
UH, BOSS...?
I THINK WE'VE GOT COMPANY.
WHAT?!
TIME FOR PLAN B!
FIRE!

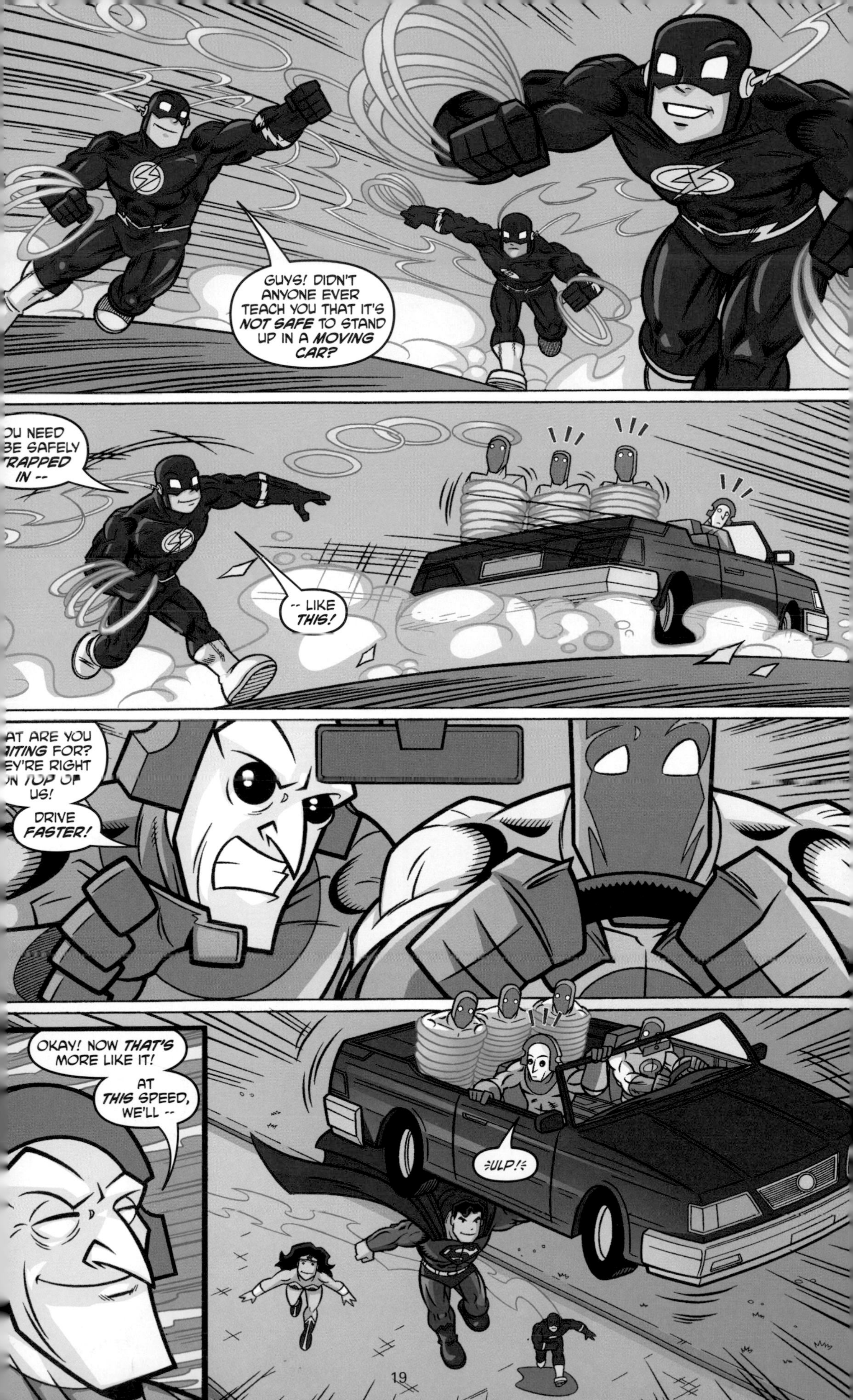
GUYS! DIDN'T ANYONE EVER TEACH YOU THAT IT'S NOT SAFE TO STAND UP IN A MOVING CAR?
OU NEED BE SAFELY TRAPPED IN --
-- LIKE THIS!
AT ARE YOU ITING FOR? EY'RE RIGHT ON TOP OF US!
DRIVE FASTER!
OKAY! NOW THAT'S MORE LIKE IT!
AT THIS SPEED, WE'LL --
ULP!

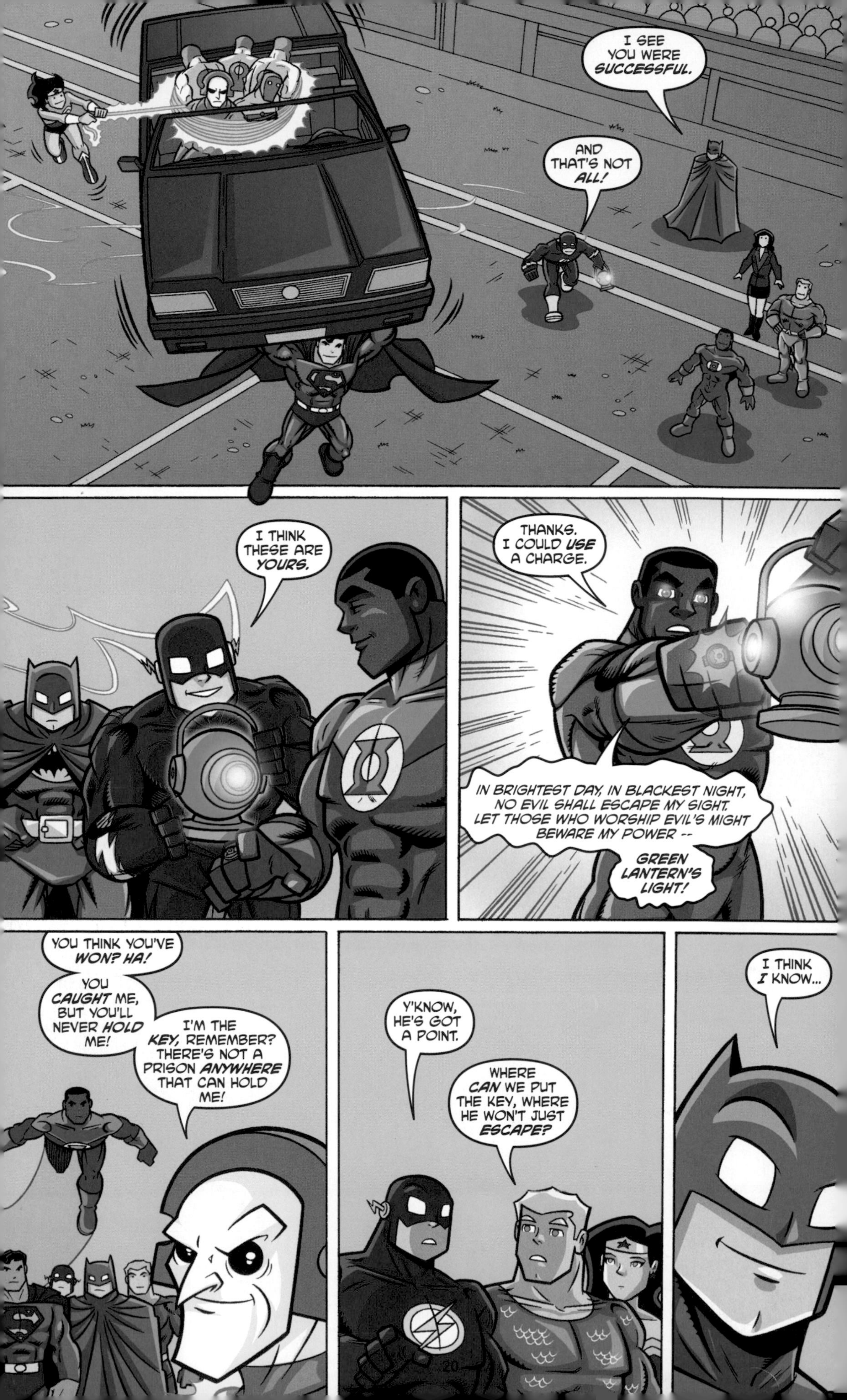
I SEE YOU WERE SUCCESSFUL.
AND THAT'S NOT ALL!
I THINK THESE ARE YOURS.
THANKS. I COULD USE A CHARGE.
IN BRIGHTEST DAY, IN BLACKEST NIGHT, NO EVIL SHALL ESCAPE MY SIGHT. LET THOSE WHO WORSHIP EVIL'S MIGHT BEWARE MY POWER --
GREEN LANTERN'S LIGHT!
YOU THINK YOU'VE WON? HA!
YOU CAUGHT ME, BUT YOU'LL NEVER HOLD ME!
I'M THE KEY, REMEMBER? THERE'S NOT A PRISON ANYWHERE THAT CAN HOLD ME!
Y'KNOW, HE'S GOT A POINT.
WHERE CAN WE PUT THE KEY, WHERE HE WON'T JUST ESCAPE?
I THINK I KNOW...

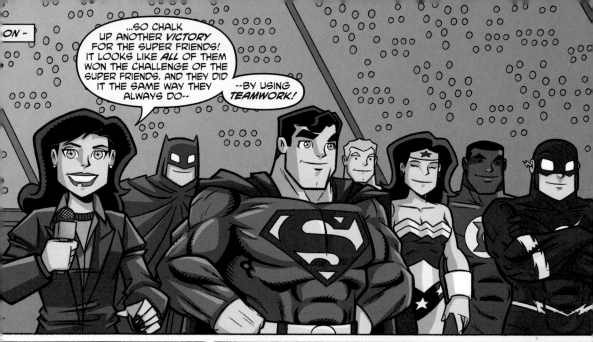

...SO CHALK UP ANOTHER *VICTORY* FOR THE SUPER FRIENDS! IT LOOKS LIKE *ALL* OF THEM WON THE CHALLENGE OF THE SUPER FRIENDS. AND THEY DID IT THE SAME WAY THEY ALWAYS DO--

--BY USING *TEAMWORK!*

ON -

THAT SHOULD HOLD HIM UNTIL *THEY* CAN BUILD A SPECIAL CELL AT THE PRISON.

HEY! LET ME *OUT* OF HERE!

HOW DID BATMAN *ESCAPE* FROM HERE?

HOW DID HE DO IT?

HOW?

ATTENTION, ALL SUPER FRIENDS!

HERE'S THIS BOOK'S SECRET MESSAGE:

PEVOY CYSOXRP ZBBU BEI CBY BINOYP

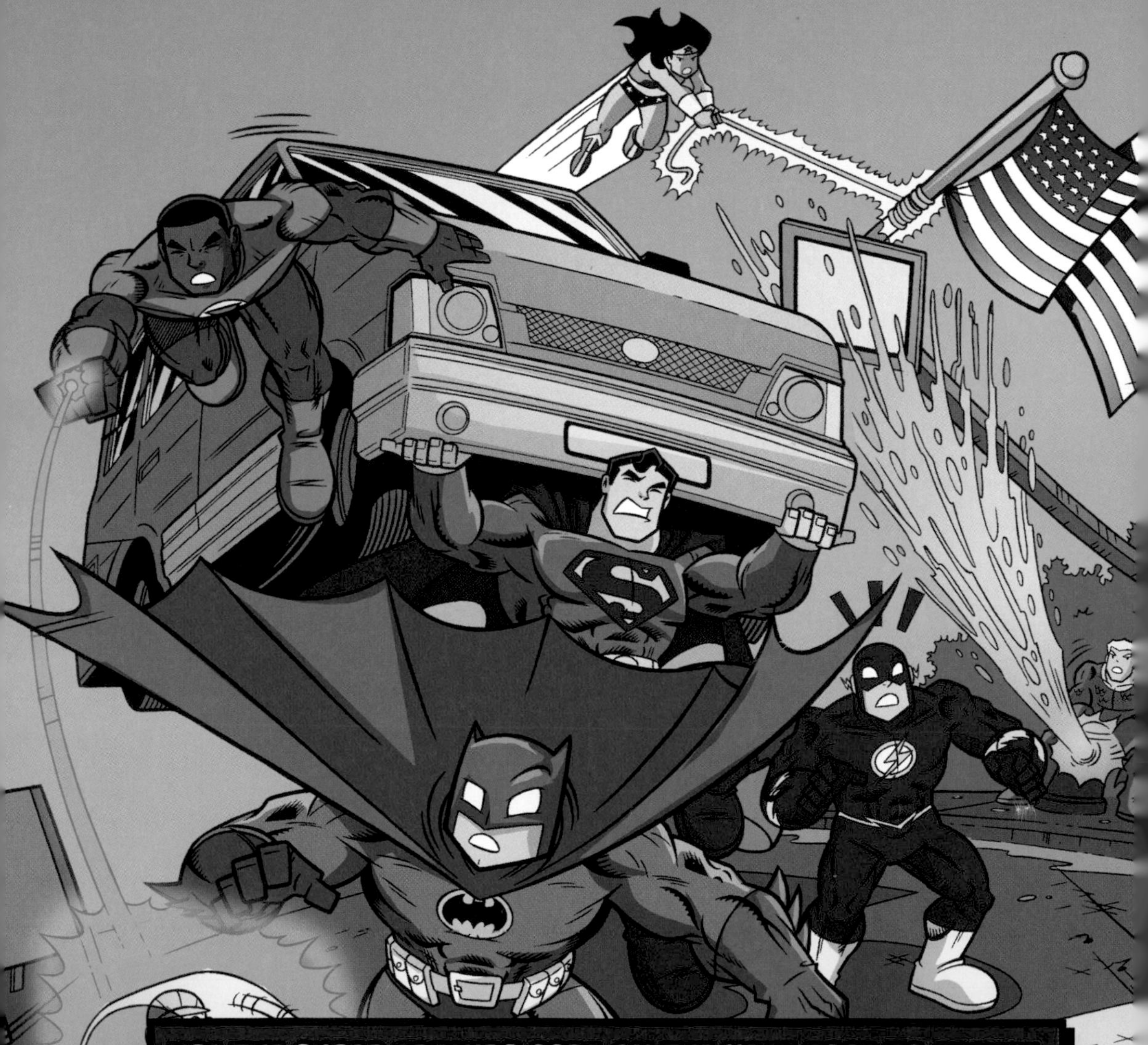

USE THE SUPER FRIENDS CODE ON THE NEXT PAGE TO FIGURE OUT WHAT THE MESSAGE SAYS AND HELP SAVE THE DAY!

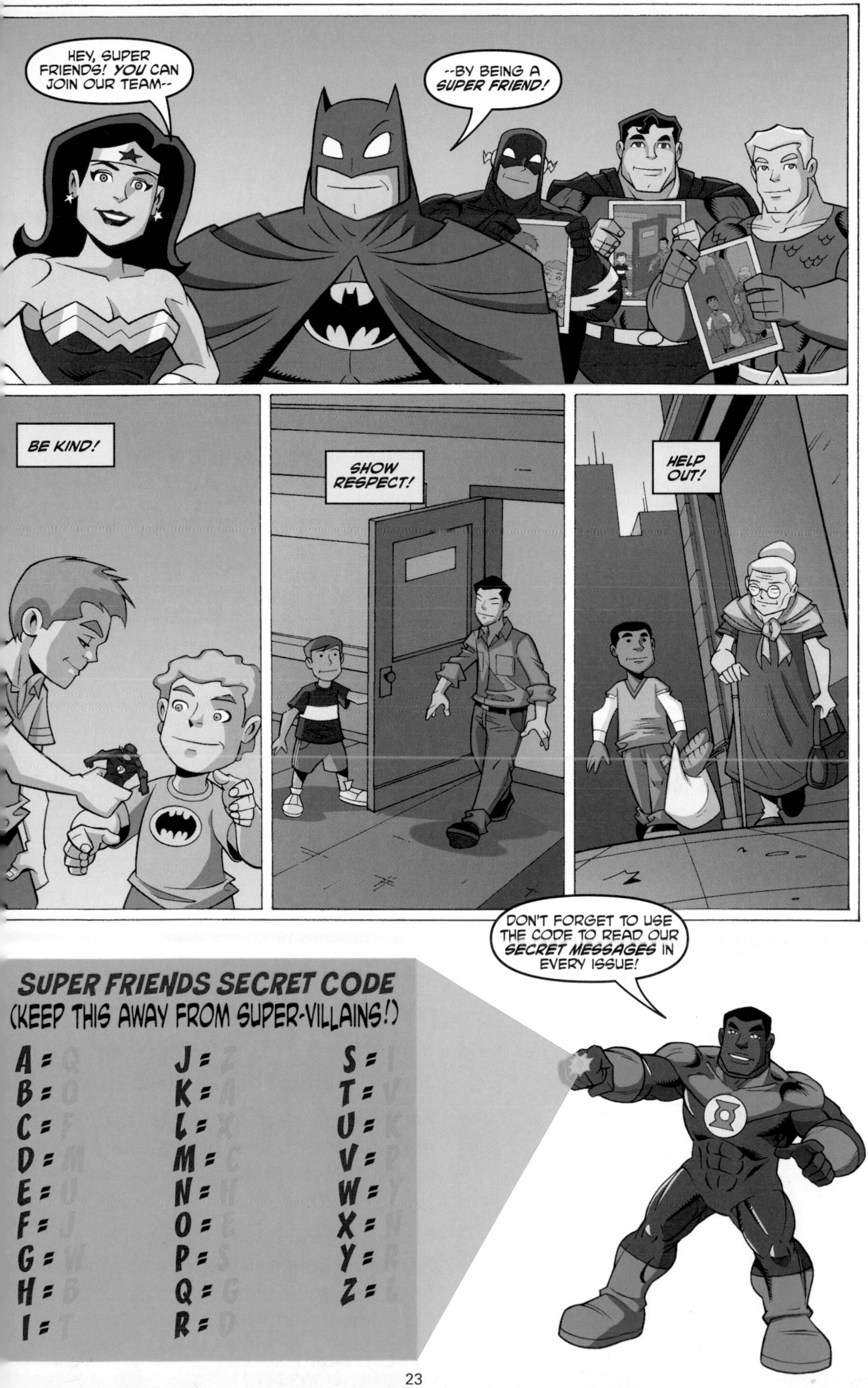

HEY, SUPER FRIENDS! *YOU* CAN JOIN OUR TEAM--
--BY BEING A *SUPER FRIEND!*
BE KIND!
SHOW RESPECT!
HELP OUT!
DON'T FORGET TO USE THE CODE TO READ OUR *SECRET MESSAGES* IN EVERY ISSUE!
SUPER FRIENDS SECRET CODE
(KEEP THIS AWAY FROM SUPER-VILLAINS!)
A = Q
B = O
C = F
D = M
E = U
F = J
G = W
H = B
I = T
J = Z
K = A
L = X
M = C
N = H
O = E
P = S
Q = G
R = D
S = I
T = V
U = K
V = P
W = Y
X = N
Y = R
Z = L

KNOW YOUR SUPER FRIENDS!

SUPERMAN

Real Name: Clark Kent

Powers: Super-strength, super-speed, flight, super-senses, heat vision, invulnerability, super-breath

Origin: Just before the planet Krypton exploded, baby Kal-EL escaped in a rocket to Earth. On Earth, he was adopted by a kind couple named Jonathan and Martha Kent.

BATMAN

Secret Identity: Bruce Wayne

Abilities: World's greatest detective, acrobat, escape artist

Origin: Orphaned at a young age, young millionaire Bruce Wayne promised to keep all people safe from crime. After training for many years, he put on costume that would scare criminals – the costume of Batman.

WONDER WOMAN

Secret Identity: Princess Diana

Powers: Super-strong, faster than normal humans, uses her bracelets as shields and magic lasso to make people tell the truth

Origin: Diana is the Princess of Paradise Island, the hidden home of the Amazons. When Diana was a baby, the Greek gods gave her special powers.

GREEN LANTERN

Secret Identity: John Stewart

Powers: Through the strength of willpower, Green Lantern's power ring can create anything he imagines

Origin: Led by the Guardians of the Universe, the Green Lantern Corps is an outer-space police force that keeps the whole universe safe. The Guardians chose John to protect Earth as our planet's Green Lantern.

THE FLASH

Secret Identity: Wally West

Powers: Flash uses his super-speed in many ways: he can run across water or up the side of a building, spin around to make a tornado, or vibrate his body to walk right through a wall

Origin: As a boy, Wally West became the super-fast Kid Flash when lightning hit a rack of chemicals that spilled on him. Today, he helps others as the Flash.

AQUAMAN

Real Name: King Orin or Arthur Curry

Powers: Breathes underwater, communicates with fish, swims at high speed, stronger than normal humans

Origin: Orin's father was a lighthouse keeper and his mother was a mermaid from the undersea land of Atlantis. As Orin grew up, he learned that he could live on land and underwater. He decided to use his powers to keep the seven seas safe as Aquaman.

CREATORS

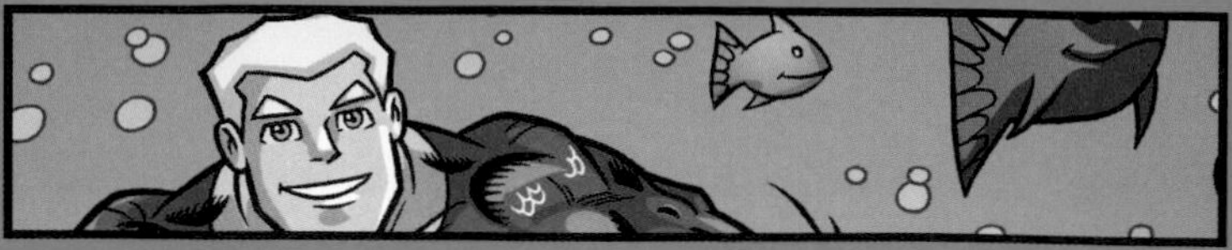

SHOLLY FISCH WRITER

Bitten by a radioactive typewriter, Sholly Fisch has spent the wee hours writing books, comics, TV scripts, and online material for more than 25 years. His comic book credits include more than 200 stories and features about characters such as Batman, Superman, Bugs Bunny, Daffy Duck, Spider-Man, and Ben 10. Currently, he writes stories for Action Comics every month, plus stories for Looney Tunes and Scooby-Doo. By day, Sholly is a mild-mannered developmental psychologist who helps to create educational TV shows, web sites, and other media for kids.

DARIO BRIZUELA ARTIST

Dario Brizuela is a professional comic book artist. He's illustrated some of today's most popular characters, including Batman, Green Lantern, Teenage Mutant Ninja Turtles, Thor, Iron Man, and Transformers. His best-known works for DC Comics include the series DC Super Friends, Justice League Unlimited, and Batman: The Brave and the Bold.

J. BONE COVER ARTIST

J.Bone is a Toronto based illustrator and comic book artist. Besides DC Super Friends, he has worked on comic books such as Spiderman: Tangled Web, Mr. Gum, Gotham Girls, and Madman Adventures. He is also the co-creator of the Alison Dare comic book series.

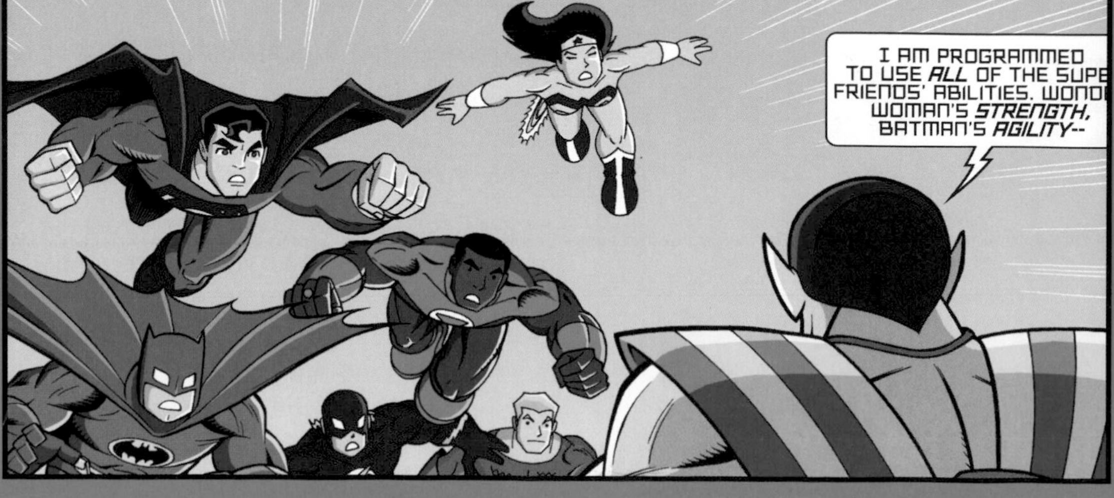
I AM PROGRAMMED TO USE ALL OF THE SUPE FRIENDS' ABILITIES. WOND WOMAN'S STRENGTH, BATMAN'S AGILITY--

GLOSSARY

abilities [uh-BIL-i-tees]–powers or skills to do things

audience [AW-dee-uhnss]–the people who watch or listen to a performance, speech, or movie

battery [BAT-uh-ree]–a container filled with chemicals that produces electrical power

charity [CHA-ruh-tee]–an organization that raises money to help people in need

condense [kuhn-DENSS]–when a gas condenses, it turns into a liquid, usually as a result of cooling

designed [di-ZINED]–created the shape or style of something

restored [ri-STORED]–brought back to the original condition

reward [ri-WARD]–something received for doing something good or useful

security [si-KYOOR-i-tee]–related to protecting people or things and keeping them safe

stupor [STOO-por]–dullness or lack of interest

telescopic vision [tel-uh-SKOP-ik VIZH-uhn]–vision that acts like a telescope, making distant objects seem larger and closer

tiara [tee-AH-ruh]–a piece of jewelry like a small crown

trophies [TROH-fees]–things taken from the enemy in victory or conquest especially when kept as proof of one's bravery or victory

villian [VIL-uhn]–a wicked or evil person

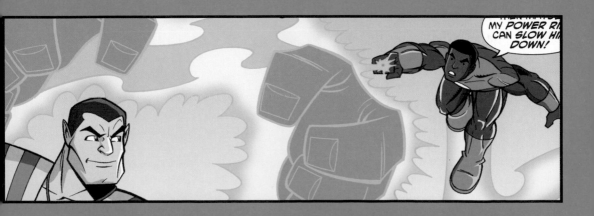

VISUAL QUESTIONS & PROMPTS

1. What is the setting of this panel? How do you know?

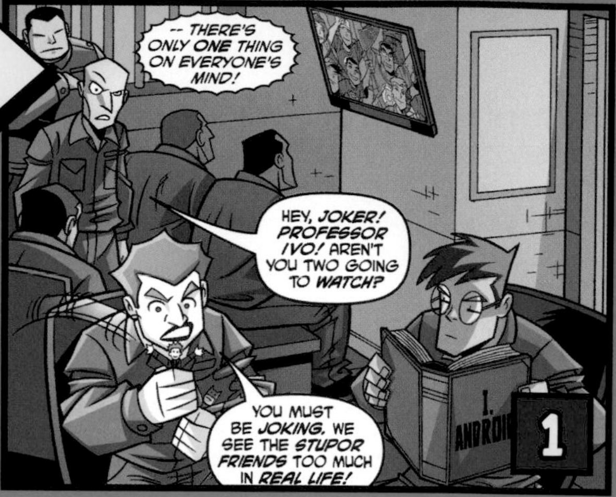
-- THERE'S ONLY ONE THING ON EVERYONE'S MIND!
HEY, JOKER! PROFESSOR IVO! AREN'T YOU TWO GOING TO WATCH?
YOU MUST BE JOKING. WE SEE THE STUPOR FRIENDS TOO MUCH IN REAL LIFE!
1

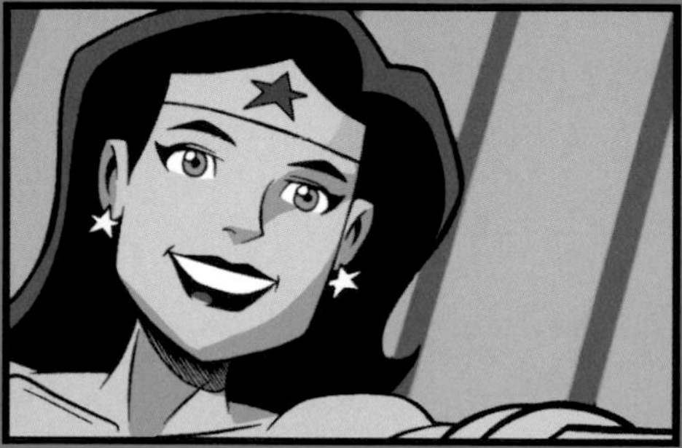

2. In comics, a character's appearance often tells the reader if the character is good or evil. Based on these panels of Superman and the Key, how do the characteristics of heros and villians differ?

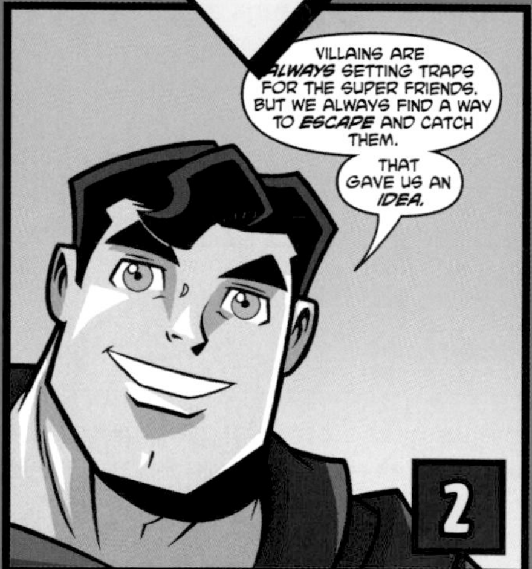
VILLAINS ARE ALWAYS SETTING TRAPS FOR THE SUPER FRIENDS. BUT WE ALWAYS FIND A WAY TO ESCAPE AND CATCH THEM.
THAT GAVE US AN IDEA.
2

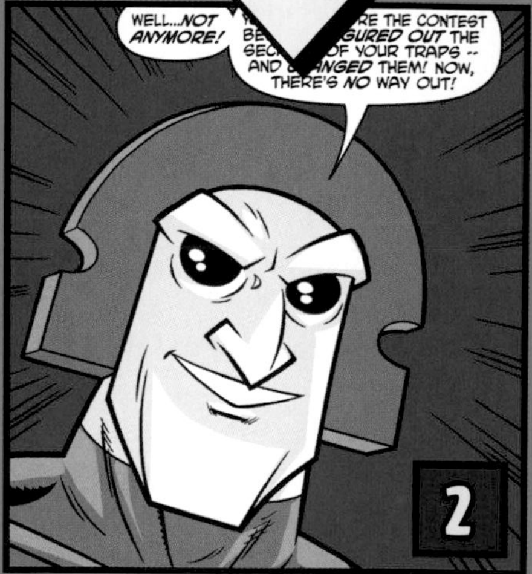
WELL...NOT ANYMORE!
2

3. Descibe how Aquaman might be feeling in this panel. What clues do you have about his health?

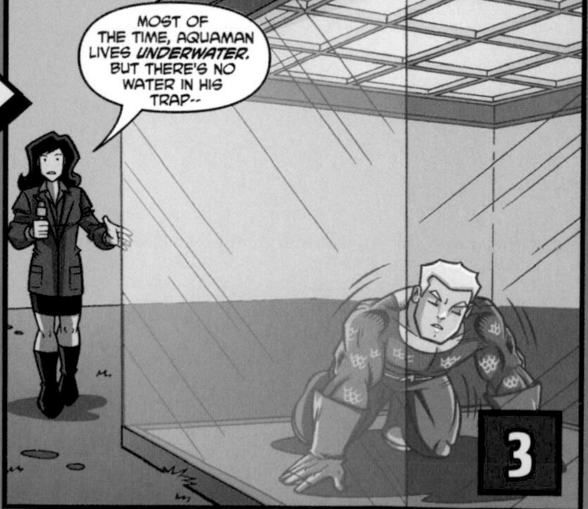
MOST OF THE TIME, AQUAMAN LIVES UNDERWATER. BUT THERE'S NO WATER IN HIS TRAP--
3

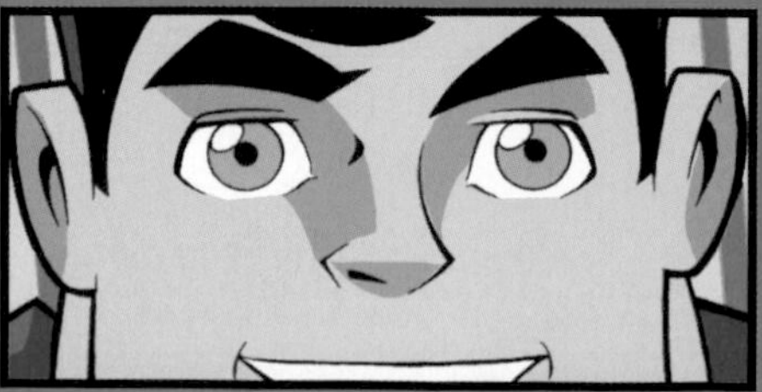

4. Often when there is fast movement or action in a panel, the artist uses a bright color for the background. Why do you think the artist makes this choice?

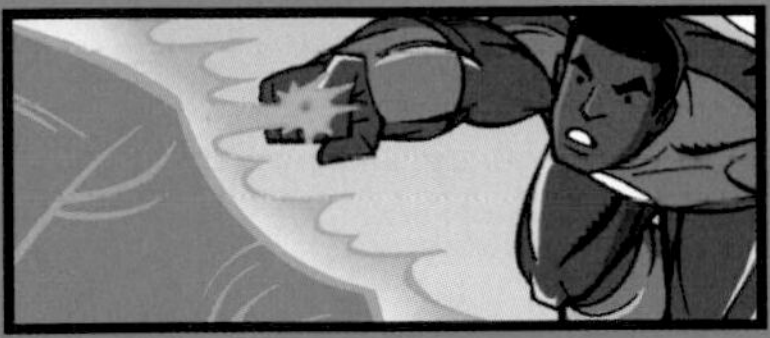

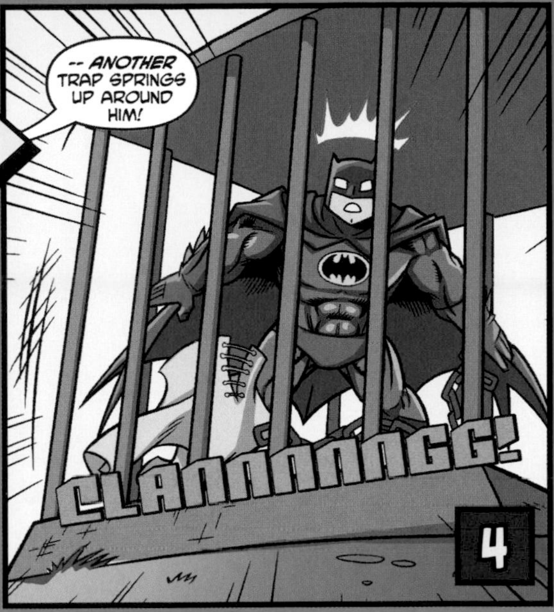
-- ANOTHER TRAP SPRINGS UP AROUND HIM!
CLANNNNNGG!
4

5. Explain what is happening here. What is the red line? What sound effects could be added to the panel?

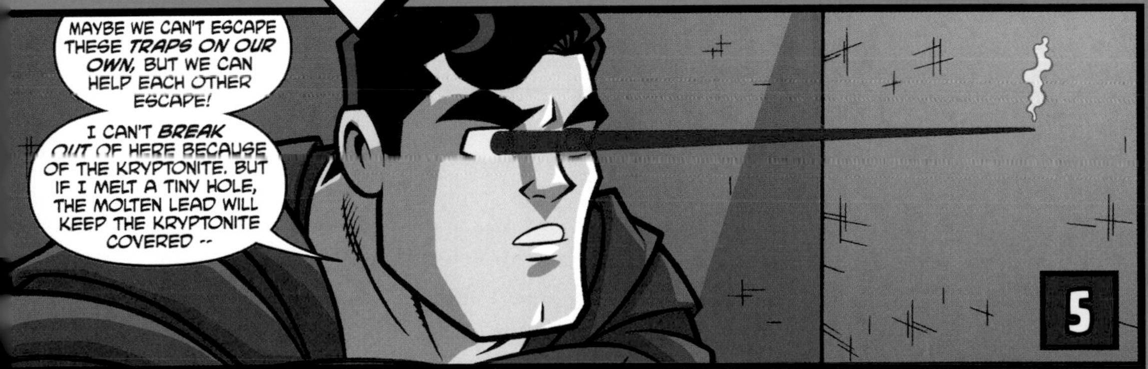
MAYBE WE CAN'T ESCAPE THESE TRAPS ON OUR OWN, BUT WE CAN HELP EACH OTHER ESCAPE!
I CAN'T BREAK OUT OF HERE BECAUSE OF THE KRYPTONITE. BUT IF I MELT A TINY HOLE, THE MOLTEN LEAD WILL KEEP THE KRYPTONITE COVERED --
5

6. Flash is shown three times in this panel. Why?

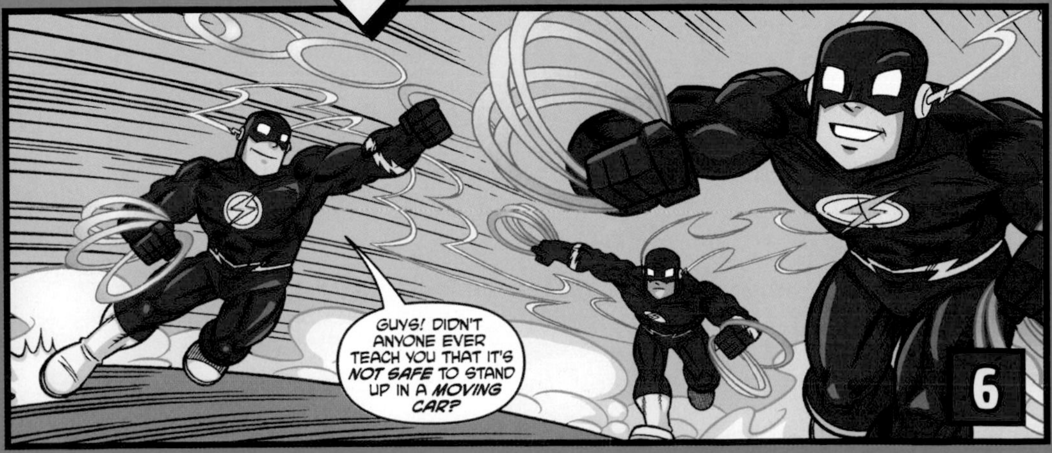
GUYS! DIDN'T ANYONE EVER TEACH YOU THAT IT'S NOT SAFE TO STAND UP IN A MOVING CAR?
6

READ THEM ALL!

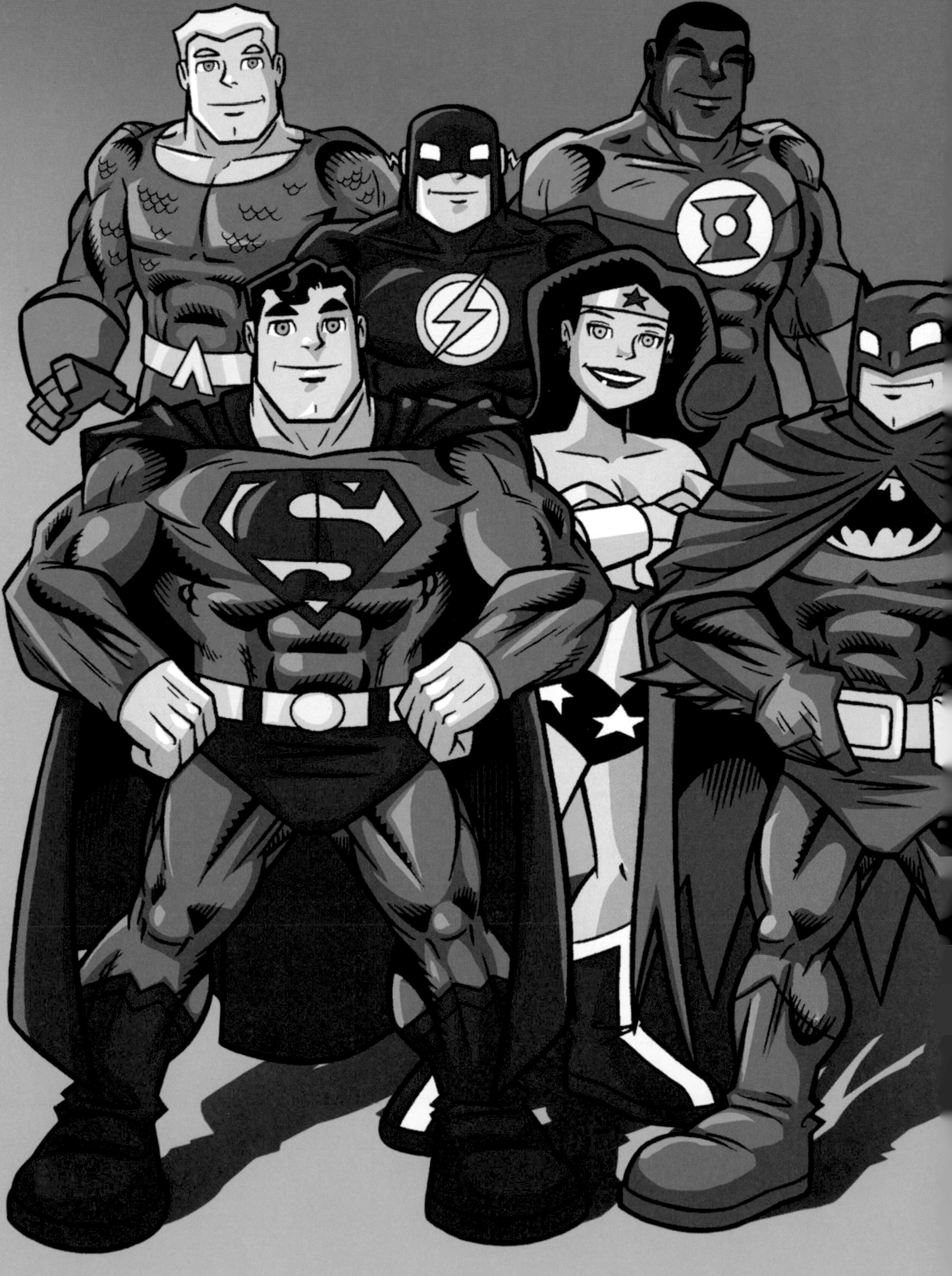

DC SUPER FRIENDS™

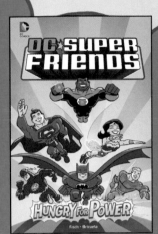

DC COMICS
DC SUPER FRIENDS
HUNGRY FOR POWER
Fisch · Brizuela

DC COMICS
DC SUPER FRIENDS
DINOSAUR ROUND-UP
Fisch · Ottolini · Staton

DC COMICS
DC SUPER FRIENDS
MONKEY BUSINESS

DC COMICS
DC SUPER FRIENDS
CHALLENGE OF THE SUPER FRIENDS
Fisch · Brizuela

DC COMICS
DC SUPER FRIENDS
APRIL FOOLS
Fisch · Brizuela

DC COMICS
DC SUPER FRIENDS
WANTED: THE SUPER FRIENDS
Fisch · McKenny · Mou

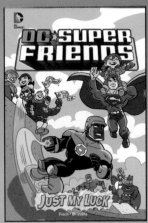

DC COMICS
DC SUPER FRIENDS
JUST MY LUCK
Fisch · Brizuela

DC COMICS
DC SUPER FRIENDS
NOTHING TO FEAR

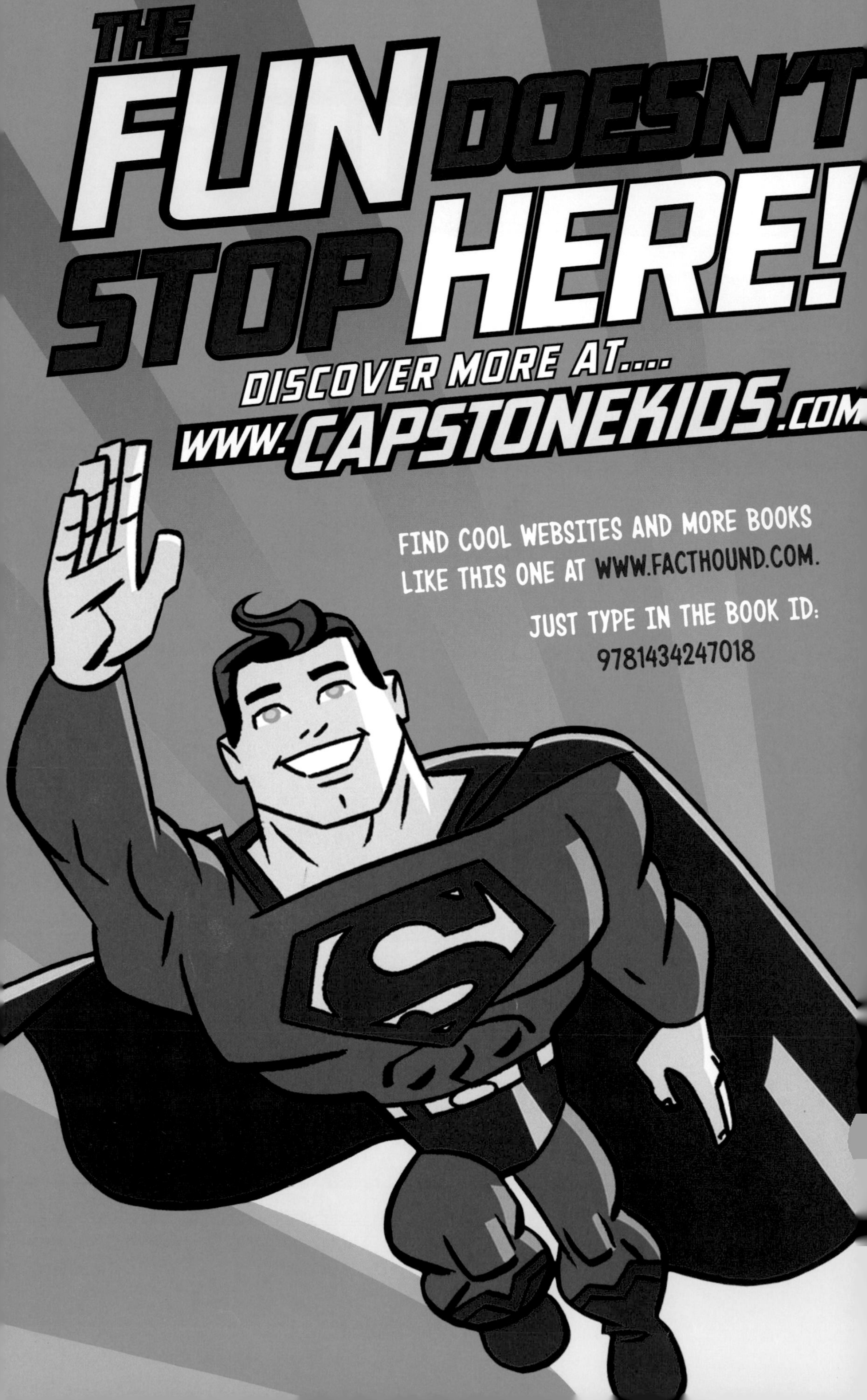
THE FUN DOESN'T STOP HERE!
DISCOVER MORE AT....
WWW.CAPSTONEKIDS.COM
FIND COOL WEBSITES AND MORE BOOKS LIKE THIS ONE AT WWW.FACTHOUND.COM.
JUST TYPE IN THE BOOK ID:
9781434247018